PRAISE ᵾᵾᴿ

LARA ADRIAN'S
New York Times and #1 internationally
best-selling vampire romance novels

MIDNIGHT BREED SERIES

"Strikingly original series...delivers an abundance of nail-biting suspenseful chills, red-hot sexy thrills, an intricately built world, and realistically complicated, conflicted protagonists..."
—Booklist on Edge of Dawn (starred review)

"Riveting...If you like romance combined with heart-stopping paranormal suspense, you're going to love this book."
—BookPage on Darker After Midnight

"One of the consistently best paranormal series out there...Adrian writes compelling stories within a larger arc that is unfolding with a refreshing lack of predictability."
—Romance Novel News

"An adrenaline-fueled, sizzlingly sexy, darkly intense...addictively readable series."
—The Chicago Tribune

"Sexy, smart and compelling. A must-read series."
—Fresh Fiction

"Equal quantities of supernatural thrills and high-impact passion. One of the best vampire series on the market!"
—Romantic Times Magazine (RT Book Reviews)

NOVELS IN THE MIDNIGHT BREED SERIES
by
Lara Adrian

The Midnight Breed Series Companion
A Touch of Midnight (prequel novella)

Kiss of Midnight
Kiss of Crimson
Midnight Awakening
Midnight Rising
Veil of Midnight
Ashes of Midnight
Shades of Midnight
Taken by Midnight
Deeper Than Midnight
A Taste of Midnight (ebook novella)
Darker After Midnight
Edge of Dawn
Crave the Night (forthcoming, 2014)

A TOUCH OF MIDNIGHT

A Midnight Breed Series Novella

(

LARA ADRIAN

ISBN: 193919394X
ISBN-13: 978-1939193940

A TOUCH OF MIDNIGHT
© 2013 by Lara Adrian, LLC

First published May 2013 in THE MIDNIGHT
BREED SERIES COMPANION

Cover design © 2013 by CrocoDesigns

This book is a work of fiction. Names, characters,
places and incidents are either products of the
author's imagination or used fictitiously. Any
resemblance to actual events, locales, or persons,
living or dead, is entirely coincidental. No part of this
publication can be reproduced or transmitted in any
form or by any means, electronic or mechanical,
without permission in writing from Author.

www.LaraAdrian.com

Available in ebook, print and unabridged
audiobook editions.

A TOUCH
OF
MIDNIGHT

DEDICATION

For every reader who asked me to share this story.

Thank you for loving Gideon and Savannah.
I hope this glimpse into their past will make you love
them even more.

CHAPTER 1

Boston University
October, 1974

Savannah Dupree turned the silver urn in her gloved hands, studying its intricate engravings through the bruise-colored tarnish that dulled the 200-year-old work of art. The floral motif tooled into the polished silver was indicative of the Rococo style of the early and mid-1700s, yet the design was conservative, much less ornate than most of the examples shown in the reference materials lying open on the study lab table in front of her.

Removing one of the soft white cotton curator's gloves meant to protect the urn from skin oils during handling, Savannah reached for one of the books. She flipped through several pages of photographed art objects, drinking vessels, serving dishes and snuff boxes from Italy, England and France, comparing their more elaborate styles to that of the urn she was trying to catalogue. She and the three other freshman Art History students seated in the university's archive room with her had been hand-picked by Professor Keaton to earn extra credit in his class by helping to log and analyze a recent estate donation of Colonial furnishings and artifacts.

She wasn't blind to the fact that the single professor had selected only female students for his after-hours extra credit project. Savannah's roommate, Rachel, had been ecstatic to have been chosen. Then again, the girl had been campaigning for Keaton's attention since the first week of class. And she'd definitely gotten noticed. Savannah glanced toward the professor's office next door, where the dark-haired man now stood at the window, talking on the phone, yet staring with blatant interest at pretty, red-haired Rachel in her tight, low-cut sweater and micro-miniskirt.

"Isn't he a fox?" she whispered to Savannah, a row of thin metal bangle bracelets clinking musically as Rachel reached up to hook her loose hair behind her ear. "He could be Burt Reynolds' brother, don't you think?"

Savannah frowned, skeptical. She glanced over at the lean man with the shoulder-length hair and overgrown moustache, and the mushroom-brown corduroy suit and open-necked satin shirt. A zodiac sign pendant glinted from within a thick nest of exposed chest hair. Fashionable or not, the look didn't do a thing for Savannah. "Sorry, Rach. I'm not seeing it. Unless Burt Reynolds has a brother in the porno business. Plus, he's too old for you. He must be close to forty, for crying out loud."

"Shut up! I think he's cute." Rachel giggled, crossing her arms under her breasts and tossing her head in a move that had Professor Keaton leaning closer to the glass, practically on the verge of drooling. "I'm gonna go see if he wants to check my work. Maybe he'll ask me to stay after school and clean his erasers or something."

"Mm-hmm. Or something," Savannah drawled through her smile, shaking her head as Rachel waggled her brows then sauntered toward the professor's office. Having come to Boston University on a full academic scholarship and the highest SAT scores across twenty-two parishes in south central Louisiana, Savannah didn't really need help bolstering her grades. She'd accepted the extra credit assignment only out of her insatiable love for history and learning.

She looked at the urn again, then retrieved another catalogue of London silver from the Colonial period and compared the piece to the ones documented on the pages. Doubting her initial analysis now, she picked up her pencil and erased what she'd first written in her notebook. The urn wasn't English in origin. *American,* she corrected. Likely crafted in New York or Philadelphia, if she were forced to guess. Or did the simplicity of the Rococo design lean more toward the work of a Boston artisan?

Savannah huffed out a sigh, frustrated by how tedious and inexact the work was proving to be. There was a better way, after all.

She knew of a far more efficient, accurate way to resolve the origins—all the hidden secrets—of these old treasures. But she couldn't very well start fondling everything with her bare hands. Not with Professor Keaton in his office a few feet away. Not with her other two classmates gathered at the table with her, working on their own items from the collection. She wouldn't dare use the peculiar skill she'd been born with.

No, she left that part of her back home in Acadiana. She wasn't about to let anyone up here in Boston think of her as some voodoo freak show. She was different enough among the predominantly white student body. She didn't want anyone knowing how truly strange she was. Aside from her only living kin—her older sister, Amelie—no one knew about Savannah's extrasensory gift, and that's how she intended to keep it.

Much as she loved Amelie, Savannah had been happy to leave the bayou behind and try to make her own path in life. A normal life. One that wasn't rooted in the swamps with a Cajun mother who'd been more than a shade eccentric, for all Savannah could recall of her, and a father who'd been a drifter, absent for all of his daughter's life, little better than a rumor, according to Amelie.

If not for Amelie, who'd practically raised her, Savannah would have belonged to no one. She still felt somehow out of place in the world, lost and searching, apart from everyone else around her. For as long as she could remember, she'd felt...*different*.

Which was probably why she was striving so hard to make her life normal.

She'd hoped moving away to attend college right out of high school would give her some sense of purpose. A feeling of belonging and direction. She'd taken the maximum load of classes and filled her evenings and weekends with a part-time job at the Boston Public Library.

Oh, shit.

A job she was going to be late for, she realized, glancing up at the clock on the wall. She was due for her 4PM shift at the library in twenty minutes—barely enough time to wrap up now and hurry her butt across town.

Savannah closed her notebook and hastily straightened up her work area at the table. Picking up the urn in her gloved hands, she carried the piece back into the archive storage room where the rest of the donated collection's catalogued furniture and art objects had been placed.

As she set the silver vessel on the shelf and put away her gloves, something caught her eye in a dim corner of the room. A long, slender case of some sort stood propped against the wall, partially concealed behind a rolled-up antique rug.

Had she and the other students missed an item?

She strode over to get a better look. Behind the bound rug was an old wooden case. About five feet in length, the container was unremarkable except for the fact that it seemed deliberately separated—hidden— from the rest of the things in the room.

What was it?

Savannah moved aside the heavy, rolled rug, struggling with its unwieldy bulk. As she leaned the rug against the perpendicular wall, she bumped the wooden case. It tipped forward suddenly, about to crash to the floor.

Panicked, Savannah lunged, shooting her arms out and using her entire body to break the case's fall. As she caught it, taking the piece down with her onto her knees, the old leather hinges holding it together snapped apart with a soft *pop-pop-pop.*

A length of cold, smooth steel tumbled out of the case and into Savannah's open hands.

Her bare hands.

The metal was a jolting chill against her palms. Heavy. Sharp-edged. Lethal.

Startled, Savannah sucked in a breath, but couldn't move fast enough to avoid the prolonged contact or the power of her gift, which stirred to life inside her.

The sword's history opened up to her, like a window into the past. A random moment, fused forever into the metal and now exploding in vivid, if scattered, detail in Savannah's mind.

She saw a man holding the weapon before him as in combat.

Tall and menacing, a mane of thick blond waves danced wildly around his head as he stared down an unseen opponent under a black-velvet, moonlit sky. His stance was unforgiving, the air about him as grim as death itself. Piercing blue eyes cut through the tendrils of sweat-dampened hair that drooped into the ruthless angles of his face and square-cut jaw.

The man was immense, thick roped muscles bulging from broad shoulders and biceps beneath the loose drape of his ecru linen shirt. Smooth, fawn-colored trousers clung to his powerful thighs as he advanced on his quarry, blade poised to kill. Whoever the man was who'd once wielded this deadly weapon, he was not some post-Elizabethan dandy, but a warrior.

Bold.

Arrogant.

Magnetic. Dangerously so.

The swordsman closed in on his target, no mercy whatsoever in the hard line of his mouth, nor in the blazing blue eyes that narrowed with unswerving intent, seeming almost to glow with some inner fury that Savannah couldn't comprehend. A dark curiosity prickled inside her, against her better instincts.

Who was this man?

Where was he from? How had he lived?

How many centuries ago must he have died?

Through the lens of her mind's eye, Savannah watched the warrior come to a halt. He stared down at the one he now met in mortal combat. His broad mouth was flat, merciless. He raised his sword arm, prepared to strike.

And then he did, driving home the blade in a swift, certain death blow.

Savannah's heart raced, pounding frantically in her breast. She could hardly breathe for the combination of fear and fascination swirling inside her.

She tried to see the swordsman's face in better detail, but his wild tangle of golden hair and the shadows of the night that surrounded him hid all but the most basic hints of his features.

And now, as so often happened with her gift, the vision was beginning to fracture apart. The image started to splinter, breaking into scattered shards.

She'd never been able to control her ability, not even when she tried. It was a powerful gift, but an elusive one too. Now was no different. Savannah struggled to hold on, but the glimpse the sword gave her was slipping...fading...drifting out of reach.

As Savannah's mind cleared, she uncurled her fingers from their grip on the blade. She stared down at the length of polished steel resting across her open palms.

She closed her eyes and tried to conjure the face of the swordsman from memory, but only the faintest impression of him remained within her grasp. Soon, even that was slipping away. Then it was gone.

He was gone.

Banished back to the past, where he belonged.

And yet, a single, nagging question pulsed through her mind, through her veins. It demanded an answer, one she had little hope of resolving.

Who was he?

CHAPTER 2

Broken glass and debris from the rotting rafters rained down in the dark as three members of the Order patrol team dropped through a filth-clouded skylight of the abandoned clothing factory in Chinatown. The surprise attack from above sent the group of feral-eyed, blood-addicted squatters in the old ruin of the building scrambling for cover.

For all the good it would do them to run.

Gideon and his two comrades had been tailing one member of this Rogue nest most of the night, waiting for the opportune moment to strike. Waiting for the suckhead to lead them to his lair, where the Order could take out not just one Bloodlust-crazed predator, but several. Half a dozen, by Gideon's quick count, as he, Dante and Conlan dropped in unannounced just after midnight.

Gideon was on one of the Rogues as soon as his boots hit the rubbish-strewn floor. He leapt after the suckhead, grabbing a fistful of the vampire's dirty trench coat as it flew out behind him like a sail. He took the Rogue down in a hard tackle, pinning it with his forearm braced against the back of the rabid male's neck. With his free hand, Gideon reached for the shorter of the two blades he wore in combat. The twelve-inch length of razor-sharp, titanium-edged steel gleamed in the scant moonlight shining in from the open roof overhead.

The Rogue began to fight and flail, snarling through its fangs as it struggled to get loose. Gideon didn't give the suckhead a chance to so much as hope it might escape him.

Shifting his hold, Gideon clutched a hank of the Rogue's unkempt brown hair and wrenched its head back. The vampire's amber eyes glowed wild and unfocused, its open maw dripping sticky saliva as it growled and hissed in the mindless fury of its Bloodlust.

Gideon plunged his dagger into the hollow at the base of the Rogue's exposed throat.

Death from the blade might have been certain enough, but the titanium—fast-acting poison to the diseased blood system of a Rogue—sealed the deal. The vampire's body convulsed as the titanium entered its bloodstream, began devouring its cells from the inside out. It wouldn't take long—mere seconds before there was nothing left but bubbling ooze, then dried-up ash. Then nothing left at all.

As the titanium did its worst on Gideon's kill, he wheeled around to gauge the situation with his comrades. Conlan was in pursuit of a suckhead who'd fled for a steel catwalk above the factory floor. The big Scot warrior dropped the Rogue with a titanium dagger shot from his hand like a bullet.

A few yards away, Dante was engaged in hand-to-hand combat with a Rogue who'd had the bad sense to think he could fight the dark-haired warrior up close and personal. Dante calmly, but swiftly, eluded every careless strike before drawing a pair of savage, curved blades from their sheaths on his hips and slicing them across the attacking Rogue's chest. The suckhead howled in sudden agony, collapsing in a boneless heap at the warrior's feet.

"Three down," Con called out in his thick brogue. "Another three to go."

Gideon nodded to his teammates. "Two heading for the back loading dock now. Don't let the bastards get away."

Conlan and Dante took off on his direction without question or hesitation. They'd run Rogue-hunting missions under Gideon's command for years, long enough to know that they could rely on his direction even in the thickest of urban combat.

Gideon sheathed his short blade in favor of his sword, the weapon he'd mastered back in London, before his travels—and his vow—brought him to Boston to seek out Lucan Thorne and pledge his arm to the Order.

Gideon swiveled his head, making a swift, sweeping search of the shadows and gloom of the old building. He saw the fourth Rogue in no time. It was fleeing toward the west side of the place, pausing here and there, ostensibly seeking a place to hide.

Gideon focused on his quarry, seeing it with something more than just his eyes. He'd been born with a much stronger gift of sight: The preternatural ability to see living energy sources through solid mass.

For most of his long existence—three-and-a-half centuries and counting—his gift had been little more than a clever trick. A useless parlor game, something he'd valued far less than his skill with a sword. Since joining the Order, he'd honed his extrasensory talent into a weapon. One that had given him new purpose in life.

His sole purpose.

He used that ability now to guide him toward his current target. The Rogue he chased must have decided better of its notion to look for cover. No longer wasting precious seconds out of motion, the feral vampire veered sharply south in the building.

Through the brick and wood and steel of the sheltering walls, Gideon watched the fiery orb of the Rogue's energy shift direction, pushing deeper into the bowels of the run-down factory. Gideon trailed its flight on silent, stealthy feet. Past a chaos of tumbled sewing stations and toppled bolts of faded, rodent-infested fabric. Around a corner into a long, debris-scattered hallway.

Empty storage rooms and dank, dark offices lined the corridor. Gideon's target had fled into the passageway before making a hasty, fatal mistake. The Rogue's energy orb hovered behind a closed door at the end of the hallway—just a few scant feet from a window that would have dumped him onto the street outside. If Bloodlust hadn't robbed the vampire of his wits, he might have eluded death tonight.

But death had found him.

Gideon approached without making a sound. He paused just outside the door, turned to face it. Then kicked the panel off its hinges with one brutal stamp of his booted foot.

The impact knocked the Rogue backward, onto its back on the littered office floor. Gideon pounced, one foot planted in the center of the feral vampire's chest, the blade of his sword resting under its chin.

"M-mercy," the beast growled, less voice than animalistic grunt. Mercy was a word that had no meaning to one of the Breed lost to Bloodlust as deeply as this creature was. Gideon had seen that firsthand. The Rogue's breath was sour, reeking of disease and the over-consumption of human blood that was its addiction. Thick spittle bubbled in its throat as the vampire's lips peeled back from enormous, yellowed fangs. "Let me...go. Have...mercy..."

Gideon stared unflinching into the feral amber eyes. He saw only savagery there. He saw blood and smoke and smoldering ruin. He saw death so horrific, it haunted him even now.

"Mercy," the Rogue hissed, even while fury crackled in its wild gaze.

Gideon didn't acknowledge the plea. With a flex of his shoulder, he thrust the sword deep, severing throat and spinal column in one thorough strike.

A quick, painless execution.

That was the limit of his mercy tonight.

CHAPTER 3

S avannah arrived early at the Art History department that next afternoon. She couldn't wait for her day's final class to let out, and made a beeline across campus as soon as English Lit 101 ended. She dashed up the three flights of stairs to the archive room outside Professor Keaton's office, excited to see she was the first student to report in for the after-class project. Dumping her book bag next to her work table, she slipped into the storage room containing the items yet to be catalogued for the university's collection.

The sword was right where she'd left it the day before, carefully returned to its wooden case in the corner of the room.

Savannah's pulse kicked as she entered and softly closed the door behind her. The beautiful old blade—and the mysterious, golden-haired warrior who'd once used it with lethal skill—had been haunting her thoughts all this time. She wanted to know more.

Needed to know more, with a compulsion too strong to resist.

She tried to ignore the little pang of guilt that stabbed her as she bypassed the bin of clean curator's gloves and sank down, bare-handed, in front of the container that held the sword.

She lifted the lid of the long box, gently laying it open. The length of polished steel gleamed. Savannah hadn't had the chance to really look at its craftsmanship yesterday, after it had fallen so unexpectedly into her hands.

She hadn't noticed then how the tooled steel grip was engraved with the image of a bird of prey swooping in for a brutal attack, its cruel beak open in a scream. Nor had she paid attention to the blade's gemstone pommel, a blood-red ruby caged by grotesque metal talons. A cold shiver ran up her arms as she studied the weapon now.

This was no hero's sword.

And still, she couldn't resist the need to know more about the man she'd watched wield it in her glimpse from before.

Savannah flexed her fingers, then gently rested them on the blade.

The vision leapt into her mind even faster than the first time.

Except this was a different peek at the weapon's past. Something unexpected, but equally intriguing in a different way.

A pair of young boys—tow-headed, identical twins—played with the sword in a torchlit stable. They could be no more than ten years old, both dressed like little seventeenth-century lords in white linen shirts, riding boots and dark blue breeches that gathered at the knee. They were laughing, taking turns with the sword, stabbing and lunging at a bale of straw, pretending to slay imaginary beasts.

Until something outside the stable startled them.

Fear filled their young faces. Their eyes went to each other, dread-filled, panicked. One of them opened his mouth in a silent scream—just as the torch on the wall of the stable went out.

Savannah recoiled from the blade. She let go of it, shaking, gripped with a marrow-deep terror for these two children. What happened to them?

She couldn't walk away. Not now.

Not until she knew.

Her fingers trembled as she brought them back over the blade again. She set her hands down on the cold steel, and waited. Though not for long.

The window to the past opened up to her like a dragon's maw, dark and jagged, an abyss licked with fire.

The stable was ablaze. Flames climbed the stalls and rafters, devouring everything in their path. Blood bathed the rough timber posts and the bale of yellow straw. So much blood. It was everywhere.

And the boys...

The pair of them lay unmoving on the floor of the stable. Their bodies were savaged, broken. Barely recognizable as the beautiful children who'd seemed so joyous and carefree. So alive.

Savannah's heart felt trapped in a vise, cold and constricted, as this awful glimpse played out before her. She wanted to look away. She didn't want to see the terrible remains of the once-beautiful, innocent twin boys.

Ah, God. The horror of it choked her.

Someone had killed those precious boys, slaughtered them.

No, not someone, she realized in that next instant.

Some *thing*.

The cloaked figure that held the sword now was built like a man—an immense, broad-shouldered wall of a man. But from within the gloom of a heavy wool hood, glowing amber eyes burned like coals set into a monstrous, inhuman face. He wasn't alone. Two others like him, dressed similarly in hooded, heavy cloaks, stood with him, parties to the carnage. She couldn't make out their features for all the shadows and the flickering, low light of the flames twisting up the walls and support beams of the stable.

Not human, her mind insisted. But if not human, then what?

Savannah tried to get a better look as the image of the boys' attackers began to waver and dissolve.

No. Look at me, damn you.

Let me see you.

But the glimpse started splintering, visual shards that broke into smaller pieces, turning this way and that. Slipping out of her grasp. Distorting what she saw.

It had to be a trick of her unsteady hold on her gift.

Because what she was seeing from this vision of the past couldn't possibly be real.

From within the deep hood of the one now holding the sword, the pair of glowing eyes blazed bright amber. And in the instant before the image vanished completely, Savannah would have sworn on her own life that she saw the bone-white glint of razor-sharp teeth.

Fangs.

What the...?

A hand came down on her shoulder. Savannah shrieked, nearly jumping out of her skin.

"Take it easy!" Rachel laughed as Savannah swung her head around. "Don't have a damn heart attack. It's just me. Jeez, you look like you just saw a ghost."

Savannah's pulse was hammering hard, her breath all but gone. She had no voice to answer her roommate, could only stare up at her mutely. Rachel's gaze went to the sword. "What are you doing in here by yourself? Where did that come from?"

Savannah cleared her throat, now that her heart had finally vacated the area. She pulled her hands away from the blade, hiding them so Rachel wouldn't see how they shook. "I...I found it yesterday."

"Is that a ruby in the handle of that thing?"

Savannah shrugged. "I think so."

"Really? Far out!" She leaned in for a better look. "Let me see it for a second."

Savannah almost warned her friend to be careful, that she wouldn't want to see what Savannah had just witnessed. But that gift—a curse, today—belonged solely to her.

Savannah watched as Rachel picked up the blade and admired it. Nothing happened to the girl. She had no inkling of the horrific past secreted in the centuries-old weapon.

"Rach...do you believe in monsters?"

"What?" She burst out laughing. "What the hell are you talking about?"

"Nothing." Savannah shook her head. "Forget it. I'm just kidding."

Rachel gripped the sword in both hands and pivoted on her heel, taking on a dramatic combat pose. Her wristful of thin metal bangle bracelets jingled together musically as she mock thrusted and parried with the blade. "You know, we shouldn't be handling this thing without gloves on. God, it's heavy. And old too."

Savannah stood up. She plunged her hands into the pockets of her flared jeans. "At least two hundred years old. Late 1600s would be my guess." More than a guess, a certainty.

"It's beautiful. Must be worth a fortune, I'll bet."

Savannah shrugged. Gave a weak nod. "I suppose."

"I don't remember seeing this on the collection's inventory list." Rachel frowned. "I'm gonna go show it to Bill. I can't believe he would've missed this."

"Bill?"

Rachel rolled her eyes. "Professor Keaton. But I can't very well call him that tonight on our date, now, can I?"

Savannah knew she was gaping, but she didn't care. Besides, it was nice having something else to think about for a moment. "You're going out with Professor Keaton?"

"Dinner and a movie," Rachel replied, practically singing the words. "He's gonna take me to that scary new one that just came out. *The Chainsaw Massacre*."

Savannah snorted. "Sounds romantic."

Rachel's answering smile was coy. "I'm sure it will be. So, don't wait up for me at the apartment tonight. If I have anything to say about it, I'm gonna be late. If

I come home at all. Now, hand me the case for this thing, will you?"

Savannah obliged, giving a slow shake of her head as Rachel donned a pair of curator's gloves and gently placed the awful weapon back inside the slim wooden box. Tossing Savannah a sly grin, the girl turned and left.

When she had gone, Savannah exhaled a pent-up breath, realizing only then how rattled she was. She reached for her own pair of gloves and the notebook she'd filed on the shelf the day before. Her hands were still unsteady. Her heart was still beating around her breast like a caged bird.

She'd seen a lot of incredible things with her gift before, but never something like this.

Never something as brutal or horrific as the slaughter of those two children.

And never something that seemed so utterly unreal as the glimpse the sword had given her at a group of creatures that could not possibly exist. Not then, or now.

She couldn't summon the courage to give a name to what she witnessed, but the cold, dark word was pounding through her veins with every frantic beat of her heart.

Vampires.

CHAPTER 4

For almost a hundred years, the city of Boston had played unwitting host to a cadre of Breed warriors who'd sworn to preserve the peace with humans and keep the existence of the vampire nation—its feral, Bloodlust-afflicted members in particular—a secret from mankind. The Order had begun in Europe in the mid-1300s with eight founding members, only two of which remained: Lucan, the Order's formidable leader, and Tegan, a stone-cold fighter who played by his own rules and answered to no one.

They, along with the rest of the cadre's current membership—Gideon, Dante, Conlan and Rio—sat gathered at a conference table in the war room of the Order's underground headquarters late that afternoon. Gideon had just reported on his team's raid of the Rogue lair the night before, and now Rio was relaying the results of his solo recon mission on a suspected nest located in Southie.

At the head of the long table to Gideon's left, the Order's black-haired Gen One leader sat in unreadable silence, his fingers steepled beneath his dark-stubbled chin as he heard the warriors' reports.

Gideon's hands were not so idle. Although his mind was fully present for the meeting, his fingers were busy tinkering with a new microcomputer prototype he'd just gotten a hold of a few days ago. The machine didn't look like much, just a briefcase-sized metal box with small toggle switches and red LED lights on the front of it, but damn if it didn't get his blood racing a bit faster through his veins. Almost as good as ashing a Rogue. Hell, it was almost as good as sex.

Not that he should remember what that was, considering how long it had been since he'd allowed himself to crave a woman. Years, at least. Decades, probably, if he really wanted to do the math. And he didn't.

While Rio wrapped up his recon report, Gideon executed a quick binary code program, using the flip toggles to load the instructions into the processor. The machine's capacity was limited, its functions even more so, but the technology of it all fascinated him and his mind was forever thirsty for new knowledge, no matter the subject.

"Good work, everyone," Lucan said, as the meeting started to wrap up. He glanced at Tegan, the big, tawny-haired warrior at the opposite end of the table. "If Rio's intel shakes out, we could be looking at a nest of upwards of a dozen suckheads. Gonna need all hands on deck down there tonight to clear the place out."

Tegan stared for a moment, green eyes as hard as gemstones. "You want me to go in, take the nest out, say so. It'll be done. But you know I work alone."

Lucan glowered back, anger flashing amber in the cool gray of his gaze. "You clear the nest, but you do it with backup. You got a death wish, deal with it on your own time."

For several long moments, the war room held an uneasy silence. Tegan's mouth twisted, his lips parting to bare just the tips of his fangs. He growled low in his throat, but he didn't escalate the power struggle any further. Good thing, because God knew if the two Gen One warriors ever went at each other in a true contest, there would be no easy victor.

Like the rest of the warriors gathered around the table, Gideon knew about the bad blood between Lucan and Tegan. It centered on a female—Tegan's long-dead Breedmate, Sorcha, who'd been taken from him back in the Order's early days. Tegan lost her first, tragically, to an enemy who turned her Minion and left her worse than dead. But it was by Lucan's hand that Sorcha perished, an act of mercy for which Tegan might never forgive him.

It was a grim but potent reminder of why most of the warriors refused to take a mate. Of those currently serving the Order, only Rio and Conlan had Breedmates. Eva and Danika were strong females; they had to be. Although the Breed was close to immortal and very hard to kill, death was a risk on every mission. And worry for Breedmates being left behind to grieve was a responsibility few of the warriors wanted to accept.

Duty permitted no distractions.

It was a tenet Gideon had learned the hard way. A mistake he couldn't take back, no matter how much he wished he could.

No matter how many Rogues he ashed, his guilt stayed with him.

On a low, muttered curse, Gideon yanked his thoughts out of the past and entered the last string of his programming code into the computer. He flipped the switch that would execute the commands, and waited.

At first nothing happened. Then...

"Bloody brilliant!" he crowed, staring in triumphant wonder as the red LED lights on the front panel of the processor illuminated in an undulating wave pattern—just as his program had instructed them to. The warriors all looked at him with varying expressions, everything from confusion to possible concern for his mental wellbeing. "Will you look at this? It's a thing of fucking beauty."

He spun the processor around on the table for them to see the technological miracle taking place before their eyes. When no one reacted, Gideon barked out an incredulous laugh. "Come on, it's remarkable. It's the bloody future."

Dante smirked from his seat across the table. "Just what we needed, Gid. A light-up bread box."

"This bread box is a not-yet-released tabletop computer." He took the metal lid off so everyone could see the boards and circuitry inside. "We're talking 8-bit processor and 256-byte memory, all in this compact design."

From farther down the table, Rio came out of a casual sprawl in his chair and leaned forward to have a better look. There was humor in his rolling Spanish accent. "Can we play *Pong* on it?" He and Dante chuckled. Even Con joined in after a moment.

"One day, you'll stand in awe of what technology will do," Gideon told them, refusing to let them dampen his excitement. No matter how big of a geek he was being. He gestured to an adjacent closet-like room where years earlier he'd begun setting up a control center of mainframes that ran many of the compound's security and surveillance systems, among other things. "I can envision a day when that room full of refrigerator-sized processors will be a proper tech lab, with enough computer power to keep a small city up and running."

"Okay, cool. Whatever you say," Dante replied. His broad mouth quirked. "But in the meantime, no *Pong*?"

Gideon gave him a one-fingered salute, smiling in spite of himself. "Wankers. Bunch of hopeless wankers."

Lucan cleared his throat and brought the meeting back on track. "We need to start ramping up patrols. I'd like nothing better than to rid Boston completely of Rogues, but that still leaves other cities in need of clean-up. Sooner or later, things keep going like they are, we're gonna need to evaluate our options."

"What are you saying, Lucan?" Rio asked. "You talking about bringing on new members?"

He gave a vague nod. "Might not be a bad idea at some point."

"The Order started with eight," Tegan said. "We've held steady at six for a long time now."

"Yeah," Lucan agreed. "But things sure as hell aren't getting any better out there. We may need more than eight of us in the long run."

Conlan braced his elbows on the edge of the table, sent a look around to everyone seated with him. "I know of a guy who'd be a good candidate as any, I reckon. Siberian-born. He's young, but he's solid. Might be worth talking to him."

Lucan grunted. "I'll keep it in mind. Right now, priority is taking care of business at home. Six Rogues ashed last night and another nest in our crosshairs is a decent place to start."

"Decent, yes," Gideon interjected. "But not nearly enough for my liking."

Rio gave a low whistle. "Only thing sharper than your mind, amigo, is your hatred for Rogues. If I ever fall, I'd not want to find myself at the end of your blade."

Gideon didn't acknowledge the observation with anything more than a grim look in his comrade's direction. He couldn't deny the depth of his need to eradicate the diseased members of their species. His enmity went back about two centuries. Back to his beginnings in London.

Dante eyed him speculatively from across the table. "Counting the suckheads you took out last night, how many kills does that make for you, Gid?"

He shrugged. "Couple hundred, give or take."

Inwardly, Gideon did a quick tally: Two-hundred and seventy-eight since coming to Boston in 1898. Another forty-six Rogues lost their heads on the edge of his sword, including the three who slaughtered his baby brothers.

He could no longer picture the boys' faces, or hear their laughter. But he could still taste the ash from the fire as he tried desperately to pull them out of the burning stable the night they were killed.

Gideon had been hunting Rogues ever since, trying to douse his guilt. Trying to find some small degree of redemption for how he'd failed to protect them.

So far?

He wasn't even close.

CHAPTER 5

Savannah took the T in to the university campus from her apartment in Allston, still groggy and in dire need of coffee. She'd had a restless night's sleep, to put it mildly. Too many disturbing dreams. Too many unsettling questions swirling in her head after what she'd witnessed by touching that damned sword. She'd been more awake than not for most of the night.

It hadn't helped that Rachel never made it home from her date with Professor Keaton. Of course, that had been her intention. Hadn't she said as much yesterday? Nevertheless, Savannah had lain awake in her bedroom of the cramped little apartment, listening for her roommate to return. Worrying that Rachel was getting in over her head with a guy like Professor Keaton, a much older man who made no secret of his willingness to play the field. Or, in his case, a large part of the female student body.

Savannah didn't want to see her friend get hurt. She knew firsthand what it felt like to be played by someone she trusted, and it was a lesson she hoped never to repeat. Besides, Rachel would probably only laugh off Savannah's concern. She'd call her a mother hen—too reserved and serious for her age—things Savannah had heard before from other people throughout her life.

Truth be told, part of her was a little envious of Rachel's free spirit. While Savannah had fretted and worried the night away, Rachel was probably having a great time with Professor Keaton. Correction: *Bill*, she amended with a roll of her eyes, trying not to imagine her roommate gasping out Professor Keaton's name in the throes of passion.

God, how she was going to get through class today without the involuntary—totally unwanted—mental picture of the pair of them naked together?

Savannah rounded the corner onto the university campus on Commonwealth Avenue, still considering the potential awkwardness of it all when the sight of police cruisers and a parked ambulance with its lights flashing in front of the Art History building stopped her short. A pair of reporters and a camera crew jumped out of a news van to push their way through a gathering crowd outside.

What on earth...?

She hurried over, a heavy dread rising in her throat. "What's going on?" she asked a fellow student toward the rear of the onlookers.

"Someone attacked one of the Art History profs in his office late last night. Sounds like he's in real bad shape."

"At least he's alive," someone else added. "More than you can say for the student who was with him."

Savannah's heart sank to her stomach, as cold as a stone. "A student?" *No, not Rachel. It couldn't be.* "Who is it?"

The reply came from another person nearby. "Some chick in his freshman Antiquities class. Rumor is they were engaged in a little extracurricular activity up in his office when the shit went down."

Savannah's feet were moving underneath her, carrying her toward the building entrance, before she even realized she was in motion. She ran inside, dodging the cops and university officials trying to keep the growing crowd outside and under control.

"Miss, no one's allowed in the building right now," one of the police officers called to her as she dashed for the stairwell. She ignored the command, racing as fast as she could up the three flights of steps and down the corridor toward Professor Keaton's office.

The news crew she saw arrive a few minutes ago hovered in the hallway, cameras rolling as the police and paramedics worked just inside the open door. As she drew nearer, a stretcher was wheeled out into the corridor with a patient being administered to by one of the ambulance attendants.

Professor Keaton lay unconscious as they pushed his gurney toward the elevators, his face and neck covered in blood, his skin bone-white above the blanket that covered him up to his chin. Savannah stood there, immobile with shock, as Keaton was whisked off to the hospital.

"Coming through!" a gruff Boston accent shouted from behind her. She jolted back to attention, and took a step aside as another gurney was pushed out of the professor's office.

There were no medics attending this patient. No urgency in the way the emergency responders wheeled the stretcher into the hallway and began an unrushed march toward the second bank of elevators. Savannah brought her hand up over her mouth to hold back the choked cry that bubbled in her throat.

Oh, Rachel. No.

Her petite body was draped completely in a sheet mottled with dark red stains. One of her arms had slid out from under the cover to hang limply over the side of the gurney. Savannah stared in mute grief, unable to tear her gaze away from that lifeless hand and the dozen-plus bangle bracelets gathered at Rachel's wrist, sticky with her blood.

Reeling in disbelief and horror, Savannah stumbled into the professor's office, her stomach folding in on itself.

"Outta here now, everybody!" one of the police detectives working inside ordered. He put a hand on Savannah's shoulder as she slumped forward and held her midsection, trying not to lose her breakfast. "Miss, you need to leave now. This is a crime scene."

"She was my roommate," Savannah murmured, tears choking her. Nausea rose at the sight of the blood that sprayed the wall near Professor Keaton's desk and sofa. "Why would someone do this? Why would they kill her?"

"That's what we're trying to find out here," the cop said, his voice taking on a more sympathetic tone. "I'm sorry about your friend, but you're gonna have to let us do our work now. I'd like to talk to you about when you last saw your roommate, so please wait outside."

As he spoke, the news crew seemed to think it was the opportune time to crowd in with their camera. The reporter inserted himself between Savannah and the officer, shoving his microphone at the detective. "Do you have any indication of what happened in here? Was it a random break-in? Robbery? Or some kind of personal attack? Should the campus be concerned for the safety of its students and faculty?"

The cop narrowed his eyes on the vulture with the mic and heaved an annoyed sigh. "Right now, we have no reason to believe anyone else is in danger. There are no signs of forced entry, nor any obvious evidence of a struggle beyond what occurred here in this office. Although it doesn't appear anything was stolen, we can't rule out theft as a motive until we've had a chance to fully review and process the scene...."

Savannah couldn't listen to any more. She drifted out of Keaton's office and into the adjacent study lab where she, Rachel and the other students had been working less than twenty-four hours ago. She dropped into a chair at one of the work tables, feeling outside her own body as the discussion of Rachel's murder and Professor Keaton's narrow escape continued in the blood-splattered office.

Savannah's gaze roamed aimlessly over the reference materials stacked on the lab tables, then over toward the archive storage room. The door was wide open, but no cops or university officials were inside.

She stood up and approached numbly, walked into the darkened room.

And even through her fog of shock and grief, she realized immediately that something wasn't right.

"It's not here."

She pivoted, a sudden surge of adrenaline sending her back to Professor Keaton's office at a near run. She made a quick visual search of the room, looking past the disheveled desk and well-worn sofa. Past all the blood.

"It's gone." The police officers and news crew went silent, everyone turning to look at her now. "Something *was* taken from here last night."

~ ~ ~

Eva had set off the compound's kitchen smoke alarm again.

The high-pitched beeping brought every warrior in the place running at full tilt to shut the bloody thing off.

Gideon abandoned his morning's work on the microcomputer—his new obsession—and hot-footed it up the serpentine corridor of the underground headquarters to the kitchen installed specifically for Eva and Danika, the only two residents biologically capable of eating anything that came out of it. Even that was questionable, when it was Rio's Breedmate's turn at the stove.

The Spaniard arrived in the kitchen mere seconds before Gideon got there. Rio had silenced the alarm and was pulling Eva into an affectionate embrace, chuckling good-naturedly as she tried to make excuses for what happened.

"I only turned away for a minute to watch something on the news," she protested, waving her hand toward the small television set on the counter as Lucan, Dante and Tegan shook their heads and returned to what they'd been doing. Conlan stayed, going over to put an arm around his mate, Danika, who stood nearby, trying to hide her smile behind her hand.

"Besides," Eva went on, "there was only a little bit of smoke this time. I swear that alarm hates me."

"It's all right, baby," Rio said around rich laughter. "Cooking has never been your best quality. Look at the upside, at least no one got hurt."

"Tell that to their breakfast," Gideon said wryly. He picked up the skillet of charred eggs and sausage from the stove and dumped the mess into the trash.

As he walked past the TV, he was struck by a pair of chocolate-brown doe eyes, fringed with feathery, thick lashes. The young woman was being interviewed outside one of the local universities. Short black curls haloed her face, a lovely, gentle face. Its soft features graced a perfect oval of smooth coffee-and-cream skin that looked like it would be as soft as velvet to the touch.

But the young beauty's mouth was tense, bracketed with stress lines on either side. And now that Gideon was looking closer, he realized tears were welled in those pretty dark eyes.

"Tell me more about the artifact you say appears to be missing," the news reporter pressed, shoving a microphone up toward her face.

"It's a sword," she answered, a voice to match her beautiful face, despite the tremor that made her words shake a bit. "It's a very old sword."

"Right," said the reporter. "And you say you're certain you saw this sword just yesterday in Professor Keaton's classroom?"

"What's this about?" Gideon asked, his gaze riveted to the young woman.

"Someone assaulted a professor at the college last night," Danika explained. "He's been taken to Mass General, critical but stable. The student who was with him was killed. Sounds like they suspect it may have been a robbery gone bad."

Gideon grunted in acknowledgment, wondering what the student being interviewed had to do with the situation.

"The sword was part of a collection of Colonial furnishings and art objects that were donated to the university recently," she told the reporter. "At least, I believe it was part of the collection. Anyway, it's missing now. It's the only thing missing, far as I can tell."

"Uh, huh. And can you describe for our viewers what the sword looks like?"

"It's English. Mid-seventeenth century," she replied with certainty. "It has an eagle or a falcon engraved into the handle."

Gideon froze, his blood running suddenly cold in his veins.

"There's a ruby in the pommel," the young woman went on, "held in place by carved steel talons."

Ah, Christ.

Gideon stood there, wooden, immobilized by the words that sank into his brain.

The weapon this student was describing in such unmistakable detail...he knew it all too well.

He'd held that very sword in his hand, a very long time ago. It vanished the night his twin brothers were murdered, taken, he assumed, by the Rogues who'd slaughtered them with it while Gideon had been away from the Darkhaven. Not there to protect them, as he should've been.

He never thought he'd see the sword again, never wanted to see it. Not after that night.

He never imagined it might end up here, in Boston.

For how long? Who had it belonged to?

More to the point, who would want it badly enough to kill for it?

The need to find answers to those questions lit his veins up with fire. He had to know more.

And as Gideon watched the pretty coed on the television screen, he knew exactly where to start looking.

CHAPTER 6

"That's the last of today's returns, Mrs. Kennefick." Savannah replaced the checkout card in the back of a popular new horror novel about a social misfit named Carrie. She eyed the book, sympathetic to the fictional high school girl from Maine who possessed some kind of frightening power. She was half-tempted to sign the novel out herself. Maybe she would have, if her day hadn't already been horrific enough.

Her supervisor, old Mrs. Kennefick, had offered to let Savannah take the night off, but the sad fact was, the last thing Savannah wanted to do was spend any more hours than necessary back home at her apartment alone. Her evening shift at the library was a welcome distraction from what happened at the university.

Rachel was dead. God, Savannah could hardly believe it. Her stomach clenched at the thought of her friend and Professor Keaton being attacked by an unknown assailant. Her eyes prickled with welling tears, but she held them back. She couldn't allow herself to cave in to her grief and shock. She'd had to excuse herself from the book return desk twice already tonight, barely making it to the ladies' room before the sobs had torn out of her throat.

If she could get through the remaining forty minutes of her shift without losing it again, it would be a miracle.

"All set then, dear?" Mrs. Kennefick patted her neat gray bun, then smoothed her similarly colored cardigan as she ambled around from her desk in the processing room.

"All set," Savannah said, adding the worn-out copy of *Carrie* to the wheeled book cart with the rest of the returns she'd handled that evening.

"Very well." The old woman took the cart and began rolling it away before Savannah could stop her. "No sense in you waiting around any longer tonight, dear. I'll go shelve these returns. Will you lock up behind you on your way out?"

"But, Mrs. Kennefick, I really don't mind—"

The woman dismissed her with a little wave and kept going, hunched over the cart, her drab-skirted behind and soft-soled shoes retreating into the quiet labyrinth of the library corridor.

Savannah glanced at the clock on the wall, watching the second hand tick slowly. She looked for something more to do there, knowing it was just an excuse to keep from returning to the reality that awaited her outside the library. She took advantage of the opportunity to organize Mrs. Kennefick's pencil cup and paperclip dispenser, even going so far as to use the edge of her long sleeved turtleneck sweater to sweep away the nonexistent dust from the pristine surface of her supervisor's desk.

Savannah was busy straightening the patron files when she felt the fine hairs at the back of her neck rise with a odd sense of awareness. A warmth prickled over her skin, strange and unsettling.

Someone was in the library's delivery room outside.

Although the adjacent room was silent, she closed the file drawer and walked out to investigate.

Someone was there, all right.

The man stood in the center of the room, facing away from her, dressed in a long black trench coat, black pants and black, heavy-soled boots. A punk, from the look of him. A very large punk.

Geez, the guy had to be six-and-a-half-feet tall and built of solid muscle. Which made it all the more incongruous to find him standing there in silent meditation, his head full of thick, spiky cropped blond hair tipped back on his broad shoulders while he perused the mural of paintings that circled a full 360 degrees around the ornately paneled, medieval-styled room.

Savannah strode toward him, cautious yet intrigued. "The library is about to close soon. Can I help you find something?"

He slowly pivoted around to face her, and, oh, wow....

The punk description might have fit his clothing style, but that's where it ended. He was handsome—devastatingly so. Under the crown of his golden hair, a broad brow and angular cheekbones combined with a square-cut jaw that would have seemed more in place on a movie screen than standing in the middle of the Abbey Room in the Boston Public Library.

"Just looking," he said after a long moment, a tinge of Britain in his deep voice.

And so he was looking, though no longer at the art. His piercing blue eyes met her gaze and held fast, so sharp and cool they seemed to read and process everything about her in an instant.

Savannah's skin felt tighter under his attention, making the soft knit of her ivory-colored turtleneck feel like sandpaper against her throat and breasts. She felt too warm, too noticed, and too aware of the sheer size and masculinity of this stranger before her.

She tried to project an air of calm and professionalism, despite the weird chaos going on with her central nervous system in reaction to this man. Striding up beside him, if only to escape his scrutiny, she glanced up at the series of fifteen original works depicting King Arthur and his Round Table Knights, painted for the library at the turn of the century by the artist Edwin Austin Abbey. "So, which are you more interested in: Abbey's work, or Arthurian legends?"

He followed her gaze up now. "I'm interested in everything. *The mind is not a vessel to be filled, but a fire to be kindled.*"

Savannah registered the statement, knew she'd heard it in class somewhere before. "Plutarch?" she guessed.

She was rewarded with a sidelong grin from the gorgeous non-punk standing next to her. "A student of philosophy, I take it."

"It's not my strongest subject, but I get by all right in most of my classes."

His smile quirked a bit at that, as if he mentally scored a point in her favor. He had a nice smile. Straight white teeth framed by full, lush lips that made her pulse kick a little. And that English accent was doing funny things to her heart rate too. "Let me guess," he said, studying her in that unnerving way again. "Wellesley? Or maybe Radcliffe?"

She shook her head at the mention of the two prestigious, private women's colleges. "BU. I'm a freshman in the Art History program."

"Art History. An unusual choice. Most of the colleges are turning out high-priced doctors and lawyers these days. Or mathematics whiz kids hoping to be the Einsteins of the future."

Savannah shrugged. "I suppose you could say I'm more comfortable with the past."

Normally, that would be one hundred percent true. But not lately. Not after what she'd seen reflected in the sword's history yesterday. Now, she wished she could go back in time and undo the touch that showed her the horrors inflicted on the pair of young boys from the past. She wished should could deny the other horror she witnessed in the blade's history too—the monsters that simply could not exist, except in the darkest kind of fiction.

She wished she could turn back the clock to the moment Rachel told her about her date with Professor Keaton, so she could warn her not to go.

Right now, after everything that had happened recently, Savannah could find no comfort in the past.

"I'm Gideon, by the way." The deep, rich voice pulled her back to the present, a welcome life line, even offered by a stranger. He held out his hand, but she couldn't muster the courage to take it.

"Savannah," she replied quietly, clasping her bare hands behind her back to resist the temptation to reach out to him, even though her gift didn't work on living things. The idea of touching him was both compelling and unsettling. She felt as if she should know him somehow, perhaps saw him at the library or around the city somewhere, yet she was certain she'd never seen him there before. "People don't generally spend a lot of time in this area of the library. The Bates Reading Room and Sargent Hall are more popular with patrons."

She was rambling, but he didn't seem to notice or care. Those arresting blue eyes watched her, studied her. She could almost sense the machinery of his mind analyzing everything she said and did. Searching for something.

"And what about you, Savannah?"

"Me?"

"Which room is your favorite?"

"Oh." She exhaled a nervous laugh, feeling stupid around him, a feeling she wasn't accustomed to. As if none of her studies or schooling could have ever prepared her for encountering someone like him. It was crazy to think it. Made no logical sense. And yet she felt it. This man—Gideon, she thought, testing the name with her mind—seemed ageless and somehow ancient at the same time. He held himself with a confidence that seemed to say little to nothing could surprise him. "This room is my favorite," she murmured dully. "I've always liked hero stories."

His mouth quirked. "Men who slay dragons? Rescue the princess in the tower?"

Savannah slanted him an arch look. "No, the quest for truth by someone who isn't afraid to pursue it, no matter the cost."

He acknowledged her parry with a slight lift of his chin. "Even if it means risking the Seat Perilous?"

Together, they glanced up at the panel depicting that part of Arthurian legend, the chair at the Round Table that would spell death to anyone taking his place there who proved unworthy of seeking the Holy Grail.

Savannah could feel Gideon studying her, despite that his gaze was fixed on the painting overhead. The heat from his big body, nearer to her than she'd noticed, seemed to burn through her clothing, imprinting itself on her skin. Her pulse ticked a bit faster as the seconds stretched out between them.

"Freshman," he said after a while, an odd pensiveness in his tone. "I didn't realize you were so young."

"I'll be nineteen in a few months," she replied, inexplicably defensive. "Why? How old did you think I was? How old are you?"

He gave a slow shake of his head. Then he brought his gaze around to look at her beside him. "I should go. As you said, the library's closing. I don't want to keep you from your work."

"It's all right if you want to stay awhile. I won't need to kick you out for another fifteen minutes, so until then, feel free to enjoy the art." She took one last look at Sir Galahad being led to the chair that would either confirm his honor or spell his doom, and couldn't help reciting another of Plutarch's quotes: *"Painting is silent poetry, and poetry is painting that speaks."*

Gideon's answering smile threatened to steal her knees out from under her. "Indeed, Savannah. Indeed it is."

She couldn't hold back her smile either. And for the first time all day, she felt relaxed. She felt happy. She felt hopeful, as odd as that seemed. Not weighted down with grief and numb with shock and confusion.

All it took was a chance meeting with a stranger, some unexpected conversation. A few moments of kindness from someone who had no inkling of what she'd been through. Someone who wandered into her workplace on a whim and ended up making the worst day of her life seem less awful simply by being in it.

"Nice to meet you, Gideon."

"Likewise, Savannah."

This time, she was the one who held out her hand. He didn't hesitate to take it. As she expected, his grip was warm and strong, his long fingers engulfing hers easily. As they broke contact, she wondered if he felt the same jolt of awareness that she did. God, their brief connection went through her like a mild electrical current, heat and energy zinging into her veins.

And she couldn't escape the fact that something about him seemed so vaguely familiar...

"I should go," he said for the second time tonight. She didn't want him to leave so soon, but she couldn't very well ask him to stay either. Could she?

"Maybe I'll see you around again sometime," she blurted, before she had the bad sense to let impulse take over her brain.

He stared at her for a long moment, but didn't respond one way or the other.

Then, like the mystery he'd been the moment she first saw him, he simply turned and strode away, out the door and into the waiting night.

~ ~ ~

Gideon waited, crouched low like a gargoyle on the rooftop corner of the library, until Savannah exited the building a few minutes later.

He meant to leave, as he'd said he would. He'd decided after talking with her for just a few minutes—after learning that she was an eighteen-year-old college freshman, for crissake—that his quest to find out more about whoever had that damned sword would need to unfold without involving a bright, innocent young woman.

He couldn't use Savannah for information.

He wouldn't use her for anything.

And he sure as hell didn't need to be lingering around her place of work, following her in stealthy silence from one rooftop to another, as she made her way from the library to the T station. But that's just what he did, telling himself it was a need to see a vulnerable female home safely in a city rife with hidden dangers.

Never mind that she might rightly count him among those dangers, if she had any idea what he truly was.

Gideon leapt down to street level to slip into the station a healthy distance behind her. He boarded a different car, watching through the crowds to make sure she was unmolested for the duration of the commute. When she got off at Lower Allston, he followed, tracking her to a modest five-story brick apartment building on a side street called Walbridge. A light went on behind a curtained window on the second floor.

He waited some more, keeping an unplanned vigil from the shadows across the way, until the dim glow of Savannah's apartment light was extinguished an hour and a half later.

Then he melted back into the darkness that was his home and battlefield.

CHAPTER 7

Art History class was cancelled that next day, of course.

The department building was quiet, no students inside today. Just professors working privately in their offices. Rumor around campus had it that Professor Keaton was expected to make a full recovery. He was still in the hospital, but someone had heard another of the professors mention that Keaton could be discharged and back to work in a couple weeks or less. It was the only good news to come out of the whole, awful situation.

Savannah only wished Rachel had been as fortunate too.

It was her friend's death that brought Savannah back to the Art History department that morning, even though there was no class to attend. She slipped inside the building, inexplicably drawn to the scene of the terrible crime.

Why had Rachel and Professor Keaton been attacked? And by whom?

The antique sword was valuable, certainly, but was it enough to warrant such a heinous, lethal assault?

As Savannah climbed the stairs to the second floor of the building, she felt a bit like she was heading for her own Seat Perilous, on a quest for a truth she wasn't certain she was prepared for, or equipped to face.

The police detectives were long gone, the barricades and tape removed from the scene. Still, simply being there put a chill in Savannah's veins as she neared Professor Keaton's office door down the hallway. But she needed to see the room again. She hoped to find something inside that she'd overlooked, something that would provide some sense of understanding of what happened, and why.

Keaton's office door was closed and locked. So was the archive and study room next door.

Shit.

Savannah jiggled the doorknob, for all the good it did. There would be no getting past the locks. Not unless she wanted to head downstairs and try to persuade one of the department professors to let her in.

Even though she made it a practice to avoid lying and manipulation, her mind started working on a host of excuses that might win her access to the rooms. She accidentally left one of her books for another class inside and needed it for an upcoming exam. She lost her student ID and thought it might be with her notebook in the study room. She needed to finish cataloguing one last item in the archive collection to make sure she got her extra credit for the project once Professor Keaton returned to school.

Right. One idea more lame than another.

Not that the honest answer would be any more convincing: She wanted to go through Professor Keaton's office and touch everything in sight with her bare hands, to see if she could pick up any clues that the police might have missed.

Deflated, Savannah started to pivot away to leave. As she turned, something caught her eye farther down the hallway on the floor. A thin circle of metal.

Could it be what she was thinking?

She hurried over to look, feeling both excited and sickened to see the delicate bangle at her feet. She recognized it immediately. One of Rachel's bracelets. It must have fallen off her wrist when they were wheeling her body away.

Savannah's whole being recoiled at the sight of the bloodstained evidence of Rachel's suffering. But she had to touch the bracelet. Whatever the tragic memento had to tell her, Savannah had to know.

She picked it up off the floor, closed her fingers around the cold metal ring.

Her extrasensory gift woke up immediately. The jolt from the bracelet overwhelmed her, the memory housed in the metal so horrifically fresh.

She saw Rachel in Keaton's office. Her face was twisted in stark, mortal terror.

And it didn't take long for Savannah to understand why....

Without warning, she was suddenly looking into the face of Rachel's attacker as the beast closed in.

And it was a beast. The same kind of fiery-eyed, fanged monster that Savannah had been trying to forget since she touched the old sword. Except this monster wasn't dressed in a hooded cloak like the group that killed the little boys. This beast wore an expensive-looking dark suit and crisp white shirt. A gentleman's refined clothes and richly styled, brown hair, but the face of a nightmarish monster.

The creature lunged for Rachel, its razor-toothed jaws open as it went for the girl's throat.

Oh, my God.

Impossible. She couldn't be seeing this, not again. It could not be real.

Was she losing her mind?

Savannah couldn't breathe. Her lungs constricted, burned in her chest. Her heart slammed hard, drumming in her ears. She couldn't find her voice, even though her entire body seemed to be screaming.

She gaped down at the bracelet now resting in her upturned palm. Every instinct told her to throw it away, as fast and as far as she could. But it was all that remained of her friend.

And the fragile ring of metal contained what might be the sole evidence of Rachel's killer.

She had to tell someone what she saw.

But who?

Her psychometry ability was outlandish enough, but to expect anyone to believe her when she tried to explain the monsters she's seen—not once, but twice—through her gift?

They would think she was crazy.

Hell, maybe she was.

Savannah's sister, Amelie, had long said their mama was a little touched in the head. Maybe Savannah was too. Because right now, that was the only thing that made sense to her. It was the only way she could explain what she had witnessed over the past couple days.

She didn't know what to do, or who to turn to.

She needed time to think.

Needed to get a grip on herself, before she lost it completely.

Savannah dropped Rachel's bracelet in her book bag and dashed out of the building.

~ ~ ~

Gideon rapped a second time on Savannah's apartment door, not at all convinced it was a good idea for him to be there.

Then again, it also hadn't exactly been stellar logic to detour from his first hour of patrol tonight and swing past the Boston Public Library in the hopes of seeing her. Nevertheless, he'd done that too, and had been troubled to learn that Savannah was absent from her shift. Bad judgment or not, he couldn't keep his boots from carrying him across town to her modest apartment.

As his knuckles dropped against the door for a third time now, he finally heard movement from inside. He'd known she was home; his talent had betrayed her to him, even though she seemed determined to ignore whoever was at the door. The peephole shadowed as she moved in front of it now to look out. Then, a soft inhalation from the other side of the door. One lock tumbled free. Then another.

Savannah opened the door, her face slack with mute surprise. Gideon drank in the sight of her in an instant, from her pretty, dark eyes and sensual mouth, to her lovely curves and lean, long limbs. Tonight she was dressed for comfort in flared jeans that hugged her hips and thighs, and white rock band tank top under an unbuttoned, faded denim work shirt.

God's balls, she was braless beneath the bright red Rolling Stones logo. The unexpected sight of her perky little breasts almost made him forget why he was there.

"Gideon." Not exactly a welcoming greeting, the way her fine black brows were knit on her forehead as she looked at him. She sent a quick glance past him to the second floor landing behind him, seeming distracted and edgy. When her attention came back to him, her frown deepened. "What are you doing here? How do you know where I live?"

He knew that bit of recon would pose a problem once he arrived, but it was a risk he'd been willing to take. "I swung past the library tonight, thought I might see you again. Your supervisor told me you had called in sick today. She seemed very concerned about you. I hope you don't mind that I came around to check in on you."

"Mrs. Kennefick gave you my address?"

She hadn't, but Gideon neither confirmed nor denied it. "Are you unwell?"

Savannah's creased brow relaxed somewhat. "I'm okay," she said, but he could see that she was flustered, nervous. There was a pale cast to her cheeks, and her face was tense, lines bracketing her mouth. "You shouldn't have come. I'm fine, but this isn't really a good time for me right now, Gideon."

Something was very wrong here. He could feel her anxiety pulsing off her in palpable waves.

Savannah's fear hung heavily in the two feet of space between them. "Something happened to you."

"Not to me." She gave a weak shake of her head, crossing her arms over herself like a shield. Her voice was quiet, small. "Something happened to my friend, Rachel, the girl I was rooming with here. She was killed a couple nights ago. She and one of the professors at BU were attacked. Professor Keaton survived, but Rachel..."

"I'm sorry about your friend," Gideon said. "I didn't realize."

It was the truth, or close enough. He hadn't known Savannah had been close to either of the victims. He could see that she was hurting, but there was something more going on too, and the warrior in him was suspicious of what else he didn't yet know about the situation.

"I did hear something on the news recently about a robbery at the Art History building on campus," he said casually. "Your friend and the professor were attacked during a break-in and theft of some type of relic, wasn't it?"

Savannah stared at him for a long moment, as if she couldn't decide whether to answer. "I'm not sure what happened that night," she finally murmured. She uncrossed her arms and moved one hand to the edge of the door. She took a step backward. The hand braced on the door now began to close it by fractions. "Thanks for checking in on me, Gideon. I'm not much in the frame of mind for talking right now, so—"

With her retreat, he advanced a pace. "What's wrong, Savannah? You can tell me."

She shook her head. "I don't want to talk about it. I can't..."

Gideon's gut tightened with concern. "You lost someone you cared about. I know that's not easy. But last night at the library, you seemed different. Not visibly upset, the way you are now. Something's scared you, Savannah. Don't try to deny it. Something happened to you today."

"No." The word came out choked, forced past her lips. "Please, Gideon. I don't want to talk about this anymore."

She was trying desperately to hold herself together, he could see that. But she was really shook up, dealing with something more visceral than simple grief or fear.

She was terrified.

He studied her closer, seeing the depth of her fright in the trembling that raked her from head to toe where she stood. Good God, what the hell could have put her in such a state?

"Savannah, did someone threaten you somehow?" His blood seethed at the thought. "Did someone hurt you?"

She shook her head, silent as she withdrew into her apartment and left him standing at the open door. He followed her inside, uninvited, but he wasn't about to walk away and leave her alone to cope with whatever had her so stricken with terror.

Gideon closed the door behind him and strode into the cramped living room. His gaze strayed toward the bedroom to the left, where a suitcase lay open on the bed, a few articles of folded clothing tossed inside.

"Are you going somewhere?"

"I need to go away for a while," she said, still drifting ahead of him into the small living space, keeping him at her back. "I need to clear my head. The only place I know where I can do that is back home in Atchafalaya. I called my sister this afternoon. Amelie thinks it's best if I come home too."

"Louisiana?" he said. "That's a bloody long way to go just to clear your head."

"It's my home. It's where I belong."

"No," he said, a clipped denial. "You're panicked about something and you're running away. I figured you to be stronger than this, Savannah. I thought you liked heroes who stood fast and pursued the truth, no matter the cost."

"You don't know the first thing about me," she shot back, and pivoted to face him. Her dark brown eyes pierced him with a hot mix of fear and anger. She crossed her arms over her chest again, a wounded, self-protective stance.

He walked toward her with unrushed strides. She held her ground, watching him approach. She wasn't retreating now, but she kept those arms braced tight against herself, barring him—maybe barring anyone—from truly getting close.

Gideon took one of her hands in a firm, but gentling, grasp. "You don't need to protect yourself against me. I'm one of the good guys."

He took hold of her other hand too now, and drew her arms down to her sides. Her breast rose and fell with each shallow, rapid breath she took as he reached up to cup her delicate jaw in his palm. Her skin was creamy smooth under the pad of his thumb, her plump lips soft as satin, the color of a dusky wine rose.

He couldn't resist the need to taste her—if just this once.

Curling his fingers around her warm nape, he brought her toward him and brushed his lips over hers. She was sweeter than he'd imagined, the heat of her mouth and the tenderness of her kiss awakening a need in him the way a thirsting man must crave cold, clear water.

Gideon couldn't keep from dragging her deeper against him, testing the seam of her lips with the hungered tip of his tongue. She let him in on a pretty moan, her hands coming up to his shoulders, clinging to him in delicious surrender.

He swept her denim shirt off so he could feel the bare skin of her arms. A mistake, that. Because now the pebbled peaks of Savannah's unbound breasts were crushed against his chest, an awareness that burned right through his black leather jacket and T-shirt, arousing him as swiftly as if she'd been standing fully naked before him.

He felt the sharp tips of his fangs elongating as desire swept through him like a wildfire. Good thing his eyes were closed, or the heated glow of his irises would betray him to her in an instant as something other than human.

Gideon growled against her mouth, telling himself this swift, dangerous passion was simply the result of a long, self-imposed drought.

Right. If only he believed that.

What he felt was something far more surprising. Troubling, too.

Because it wasn't just any woman he wanted in that moment. It was this one only.

Maybe she sensed the dark strength of his need for her. God knew, she had to feel it. His cock was a ridge of steel between them, his veins pulsing with a drumming demand to take her. To claim her.

"Gideon, I can't." She broke away and sucked in a hitching breath. Her fist came up to her mouth, pressing against her glistening, kiss-swollen lips. "I'm sorry, I can't do this," she whispered brokenly. "I can't start wanting something that feels so right when everything else around me feels so terribly wrong. I'm just so confused."

Hell, he was too. Confusion was a wholly unfamiliar feeling for him. This woman had knocked him off his axis the moment he met her, from her quick-witted comebacks at the library, to the intense attraction she stirred in him, just to be near her.

He hadn't come to her apartment looking to seduce her, but now that he'd kissed her, he wanted her. Badly. Their kiss left a fierce desire pounding through him for the first time in more years than he cared to recall. It took all his self-control to cool the hammering of his pulse, to make sure the amber was extinguished from his eyes before he met her gaze. To coax his fangs back to their human-like state before he attempted to speak.

Savannah heaved a sigh. "I've never been so confused in all my life. And you're right, Gideon. I am scared." She looked so vulnerable and sweet. So alone. "I'm scared that I'm going crazy."

He stepped closer, gave a mild shake of his head. "You don't seem crazy to me."

"You don't know," she replied, her voice quiet. "Nobody knows, except for Amelie."

"Nobody knows what, Savannah?"

"That I...see things." She let the statement hang between them for a long moment, her gaze searching his eyes, watching his face for a reaction. "I saw the attack on Rachel. I saw how she was murdered. I saw...the monster that did it."

Gideon held himself still at her mention of the word *monster*. He kept his expression neutral, a carefully schooled show of outward calm and patient understanding, despite that inside his Breed instincts were on full-alert, alarm bells clanging. "What do you mean, you saw your friend's killing? You were there?"

She slowly shook her head. "I saw it afterward, when I found one of Rachel's bracelets outside Professor Keaton's office. She was wearing it that night. I touched the bracelet, and it showed me everything." Her lips pressed together, as though she wasn't sure she should go on. "I can't explain how or why, but when I touch an object...I can see a glimpse of its past."

"And when you touched her bracelet, you saw your friend's death."

"Yes." Savannah stared at him with a gaze that was far too wise. Bleak with a dark, unswerving knowledge. "I saw Rachel being murdered by something inhuman, Gideon. It looked like a man, but it couldn't have been. Not with sharp fangs and hideous glowing yellow eyes."

Holy. Bloody. Hell.

Forgetting the fact that she had just confessed to having a powerful extrasensory ability—something many mortals faked but very few genuinely possessed—it was Savannah's other revelation that had Gideon's veins going tight and cold as she spoke.

When he didn't answer right away, Savannah blew out a humorless laugh. "Now you do think I'm crazy."

"No." No, he didn't think she was crazy. Far from it. She was intelligent and beautiful, a hundred years of wisdom in those soft brown eyes that hadn't even seen twenty years of life yet. She was extraordinary, and now Gideon wondered if there was something more to Savannah that he had yet to understand.

But before he could pose the questions— questions about her ESP talent and whether her body bore any unusual birthmarks—she turned away from him and the answer was right there in his line of sight. A small red mark on her left shoulder blade, only partially visible beneath the thin strap of her white tank top. It was unmistakable: a teardrop falling into the cradle of a crescent moon.

Savannah wasn't merely human.

She was a Breedmate.

Ah, fuck. This wasn't good. Not good at all. There was a protocol to be observed when it came to the discovery of women like Savannah living among the *Homo Sapiens* public at large. That protocol certainly didn't include seduction or duplicity, two things Gideon was currently teetering between like a man on a high wire.

"Since I've obviously rendered you mute with my mental instability," she went on, as his uncharacteristic loss for words or a quick solution eluded him, "then I might as well tell you about the other glimpse I saw. There was a sword in the Art History's collection, a very old sword. The one item that went missing the other night. I touched that sword recently too, Gideon." She turned back to look at him. "It showed me the same kind of creature—a group of them, in fact. Using that sword, they slaughtered a pair of little boys a long time ago. I'd never seen anything so awful. Not until I saw what happened to Rachel. I know you probably don't believe any of this...."

"I believe you, Savannah." His mind churned on the implications of everything he was hearing, everything he was seeing in this frightened, but forthright, female. "I believe you, and I want to help you."

"How can you help?" He heard the desperation edging into her voice now. She was exhausted, emotionally drained. She drifted over to the sagging sofa and dropped down onto it Bent over her knees, she held her head in her hands. "How can anyone help with something like this? I mean, there's no possible way that what I saw is real. It doesn't make any sense, right?"

God help him, he nearly blurted out the truth to her, right then and there. He wanted to explain away her confusion, help her make sense of everything that had her so distressed and uncertain now.

But he couldn't. He didn't have that right.

The Order needed to be informed of Savannah's existence. As a warrior—hell, like any other member of the Breed race—Gideon was duty-bound to see this female gently introduced to their world and her place within it, should she choose to take part. Not plunged carelessly into the worst of it.

"What I saw doesn't make sense," she murmured. "But maybe I should go to the police and tell them anyway."

"You can't do that, Savannah." His words came out too quickly, too forcefully. It was a command, and he couldn't take it back.

Her head came up then, her brow creased in a frown. "I have to tell someone, don't I?"

"You did. You told me." He walked over, sat down beside her on the sofa. She didn't flinch or withdraw when he put his hand on her back and slowly caressed her. "Let me help you through this."

"How?"

He reached up with his free hand to stroke the velvet curve of her cheek. "For now, I just need you to trust me that I can."

She held his gaze for a long moment, then gave a nod and curled into his embrace. Her head rested over his heart, her slender body nestled close, warm and soft in his arms. It was a struggle to hold his desire in check with Savannah pressed so sweetly against him.

But she needed comfort now. She needed to feel safe. He could give her that, at least for the moment.

Gideon held her as she fell into a hard sleep in his arms. Sometime later, easily hours, he lifted her off the sofa and carried her tenderly to her bed so she could rest more comfortably.

He stayed until the hour before dawn, watching over her. Making sure she was safe.

Wondering what the hell he was getting himself into.

CHAPTER 8

"Tell me this is some kind of fucking joke."

Lucan Thorne wasn't at all pleased to hear that Gideon had gone AWOL from the night's patrol. He'd been even less enthused to learn where Gideon had spent those off-grid hours.

"A goddamn Breedmate? What the hell were you thinking, man?" The Gen One leader of the Order blew out a nasty curse. "Maybe you weren't thinking. Not with your brain, anyway. That alone is cause for serious concern, if you ask me. You've never lost sight of your duty to the Order, Gideon. Not once in all these years."

"Nor have I lost sight of it now."

He was seated in the war room with Lucan and Tegan, the former radiating fury and pacing the room like a caged cat. The latter was sprawled in a conference chair at the other end of the table, showing less than passing interest in Gideon's

62

morning-after ass-chewing while idly spinning a pen around on top of a mission review notebook.

"My interest in this woman has nothing to do with Order objectives. I told you, it's personal."

"Exactly my point." Lucan's stormy gray eyes narrowed on him. "Personal agendas have no place in this operation. Personal agendas make people sloppy. You get sloppy, you get people killed."

"I can handle this, Lucan."

"Not your choice, Gid. You know the protocol. We have to let the Darkhavens know about her, let them step in on this. We don't do diplomatic work. For damn good reason."

"She witnessed a Breed assault on a human," Gideon blurted. "The coed who ended up in the morgue after the attack on her and one of the professors over at the university the other night. The dead girl was Savannah's roommate. She was killed by one of our kind."

Lucan's jaw went even more rigid. "You're certain of this? You're saying this Breedmate—Savannah— was there when it happened?"

"Her talent, Lucan. It's psychometry. She touches an object and can see a bit of its past. That's how she saw her friend's killing."

"She tell anyone about this?" Tegan drawled from his seat at the end of the table.

"No. Only me," Gideon replied. "I'd like to keep it that way—for her own sake and that of our entire race. And that's not all she's seen with her gift."

Both Gen One warriors stared at him now.

"This shit is about to get even worse?" Lucan growled.

"During the attack, there was a sword taken from the university's Art History archives. A sword I'm very familiar with, because it was the one a band of Rogues turned on my young brothers the night they were slaughtered outside our family Darkhaven in London." Gideon cleared his throat, still tasting the smoke that lingered for months after the stable was torched. "Savannah touched this sword too. She saw the Rogues and what they did to my kin. I never gave that damned sword another thought, until now. Until I realized it had surfaced in Boston, some three hundred years later."

Tegan grunted. "Surfaced, only to disappear again."

"That's right. I need to know who has that blade now."

Tegan gave a vague nod, his overlong tawny hair falling over his eyes, but not quite masking the intensity of his gem-green gaze. "You think there's a connection between the sword being here in Boston and the murders of your brothers centuries ago."

"It's a question that needs to be answered," Gideon said. "And I can't do that unless Savannah can identify the Breed male responsible for the attack at the university."

"What about the other victim, the one who survived?" Lucan said. "That's another potential witness who was actually there and lived to tell."

Gideon shook his head. "He's still hospitalized, critical. In the time it takes him to come around enough for some private questioning and the requisite memory scrub afterward, Savannah could have already given me everything I need."

Although Lucan didn't say as much, Gideon could see the suspicion in the Gen One's keen eyes. "You're risking too much, letting yourself get close to this female. She's a Breedmate, Gideon. That might be all right for guys like Con and Rio, but for any of us?" He glanced to Tegan, then back to Gideon. "We're the longest-standing members of this operation now. We're the core. We've each been through enough shit to know that relationships, blood bonds, don't mix well with warfare. Someone always gets hurt in the end."

"I'm not looking for a mate, for fuck's sake." Gideon's reply was sharp, sounding too defensive, even to his own ears. He exhaled a ripe oath. "And I have no intention of hurting her."

"Good," Lucan said. "Then you'll have no problem when I arrange to have one of the Darkhavens meet the female at her apartment and take her into their protective custody while she's being brought up to speed on the Breed and her place in our world."

Gideon bristled, coming up out of his chair to face off with his old friend and the Order's commander. "Trance her and dump her with one of the Boston Darkhaven leaders? Not a chance. She's just a scared, confused kid, Lucan."

"You're not acting like she's just a kid. You're acting like you're responsible for this female. Like you've already got more than a passing interest."

Christ, did he? Gideon wanted to refute the accusation, but the words sat like cold lead in the back of his throat.

He hadn't intended to feel anything for Savannah. He sure as hell didn't expect to feel the sudden, violent spike of possessiveness over her at the mere idea of walking away now, leaving her safety and wellbeing in the care of the Breed's civilian arm.

Nor could he ever have imagined the day when he'd be standing off against Lucan Thorne over any direct command, let alone a command that Gideon knew in his gut was the right call for Lucan to make. For Savannah's sake, if nothing else.

Lucan fixed Gideon with a grim stare. "She's out there right now, walking around with the word vampire on the tip of her tongue. How many people do you think she'll tell before we have the chance to contain her? She told you, for crissake. What if she tells the police next?"

"She won't," Gideon said, wishing he believed it. "I told her I would help her sort everything out. I told her she could trust me."

"Trust you? She just met you," Lucan pointed out. "She's got friends she could tell this tale to, classmates. Family?"

Gideon nodded. "A sister in Louisiana. I don't know about anyone else. But I can find out. I can take care of any loose threads. I want to be the one to explain everything to Savannah. After last night, I owe her that."

Lucan grunted, his expression stony, unconvinced.

Gideon pressed on. "I want to know what the sword that was used to slay my brothers is doing here in Boston. I want to know who has it, and why. I should think the Order would like that answer too, seeing how the son of a bitch in question murdered one human to get it and left another near death."

"We can't leave her out there on her own, Gid. Her knowledge is a threat to the entire Breed nation. It's also a threat to her, if the one who killed her roommate somehow learns there was a witness and turns his sights on Savannah."

Gideon's veins turned to ice at the thought. He would eviscerate any Breed male who so much as touched her with intent to harm. "I'm not about to let anyone hurt her. She needs to be protected."

"Agreed," Lucan said. "But that means day and night, something we can't enforce so long as she's living among the human population. And we sure as hell aren't bringing a civilian female here to the compound." Lucan stared, a tendon ticking in his square jaw. "You want to initiate her about the Breed and our world, fine. I'll give you that. You want to see if her talent can help us ID the bastard who attacked those humans the other night, that's yours too."

Gideon nodded, grateful for the chance and more relieved than he should have been at the prospect of Savannah being entrusted to his care.

Lucan cleared his throat pointedly. "You bring her up to speed. You question her. But you'll do all of this inside the secured shelter of a local Darkhaven. It's the best place for her right now, Gideon. You know that."

He did. But that didn't mean he had to like it.

And he didn't like it.

At the moment, he didn't see any better options.

"I'll make some calls," Lucan said. "This plan goes into motion tonight."

Gideon remained standing, his molars clamped together, fists curled at his sides as the Order's leader left the room. Tegan got up from his chair a moment later. He prowled toward Gideon, studying him with those unreadable eyes. He held something in his hand—a folded piece of paper, torn from the notebook that lay on the table alongside the pen he'd been toying with during the impromptu meeting.

"What's this?" Gideon said as the big Gen One offered the square of note paper to him.

Tegan didn't answer.

He strode out of the war room and headed down the corridor without a word.

~ ~ ~

The university campus was crowded with students that next day at noontime, people seated in small groups under tall, leafy oaks, eating packed lunches, others playing sports on the broad, green lawns. It seemed practically everyone was taking advantage of a sunny and warm October day. A pretty snapshot of a world that seemed so innocent. So...normal.

Savannah strolled past her chattering, laughing, carefree classmates, her steps hurried on the concrete sidewalk, her arms wrapped tightly around her book bag.

She had just left a meeting with her academic advisor, who'd given her clearance for a short leave of absence from her classes. She was going home soon, leaving in several hours. Although she'd told the advisor she expected to return to class in a couple of weeks, after she dealt with some "personal issues," Savannah wasn't sure there was enough time in the world to come to terms with everything she'd seen over the past few days.

She still wondered if she were somehow losing her mind. Gideon hadn't seemed to think so last night. It had been incredibly sweet of him to check in on her, concerned that she had called in sick from work. His comfort, although totally uninvited and unexpected, had been just what she needed.

His kiss hadn't been half bad either. More like, incredible. She hadn't been prepared for how good it felt to be in his arms, her mouth under his control. If she concentrated, she could still feel the heat of his lips on hers. And her body remembered too, every nerve ending going tingly and warm at just the thought of being wrapped up in him.

If Gideon were a lesser man, he might have used her shaky emotional state to his advantage last night and tried to get into her pants. God knew, after the kiss they shared, she likely wouldn't have needed much convincing to let him take things further.

She had actually dreamt he stayed with her most of the night. But there was no sign of him when she woke up alone this morning in her bed, still dressed in her tank top and jeans.

Would she see him again?

Probably not very likely. She had no idea how to reach him. No idea where he lived, or what he did for a living. She didn't even know his full name. Somehow, since their first chance meeting, he had managed to avoid revealing her a single thing of significance about himself, other than the facts that he was obviously well-read and well-educated.

Not to mention endlessly patient and understanding when it came to hysterical women going off about woo-woo ESP abilities and supernatural creatures that couldn't possibly exist outside slasher films and horror novels.

Gideon had been more than patient or understanding, in fact. He'd been a source of calm for her, more supportive than she ever could have hoped. Some part of her believed him when he said he could help her figure everything out. That he wanted to help her make sense of what she'd told him, even though inwardly he had to suspect she was more than a little touched.

There was a part of her that believed Gideon to be capable of anything he said, anything he promised. He simply projected that air of total, unswerving command. He filled any room he was in, radiated an indefinable power. His intelligent blue eyes told anyone who looked in them that he possessed the wit and experience of a man twice his age.

Just how old was he, anyway?

Savannah had mentally placed him around thirty, but she couldn't be certain. He never did answer when she asked him his age that first night in the library. He seemed too worldly, too wise somehow, to be older than her by just a decade-plus. He had to be much older than she had assumed, yet his face had no lines, no scars or blemishes to betray his years.

And his body...it felt built of solid muscle and strong, unbreakable bone. Ageless, like so much else about him.

And now that she was thinking about it, there was something distantly, oddly familiar about Gideon too. She looked at him and felt a niggling of her senses, as if they'd met somewhere before, impossible though it was.

Despite the enthusiasm of her instincts—or other parts of her anatomy—she was positive the first time she'd ever met Gideon was two nights ago in the Abbey Room of the Boston Public Library. Until two nights ago, he'd been a stranger to her. A stranger who didn't deserve to have her problems, real or imagined, dumped on him.

Which is why, when Amelie called early that morning to tell Savannah she'd purchased a bus ticket home for her and had it waiting at the station for her later that evening, Savannah had agreed it was probably best for her to return to Louisiana for a while.

She had one more appointment to take care of on campus, then she would be going back to her apartment to finish packing. She wished there was a way for her to see Gideon before she left, say goodbye at least. But short of camping out at the library in the hopes that he might show up there again this afternoon, she had no means of locating him before she had to leave for the bus station tonight.

Maybe Mrs. Kennefick knew more about him? She'd worked in the library records room all her adult life; if Gideon was a patron, maybe Mrs. Kennefick could give Savannah his full name or address. It was a place to start, anyway. Savannah could call and ask as soon as she wrapped up at the English department.

The thought put such a current of hope through her veins, Savannah hardly noticed the white Firebird rolling up behind her at a slow crawl on the street parallel to her on the sidewalk. The passenger side window was rolled down, disco music sifting out from the car.

71

Annoyed, Savannah glanced over, squinting in the sunlight as the driver reduced his speed even more to keep pace with her.

He was the last person she expected to see today. "Professor Keaton?"

"Savannah. How are you?"

"Me?" she asked, incredulous. He braked to a stop and leaned across the seats as she bent and peered to have a closer look at him. "I'm okay, but what about you? What are you doing out of the hospital? I heard you weren't expected to be released for a week or more."

"Been out for the past hour. Thank God for the miracle of modern medicine." His smile seemed weak, not quite reaching his eyes. He appeared pale and wan, his tanned skin kind of waxy against the dark color of his moustache and heavy brows. He looked haggard and exhausted, like a clubber coming off a rough weekend bender.

And no wonder—two nights ago the man had been hauled away unconscious to the ICU. Now he was behind the wheel of his muscle car with Barry White crooning through the speakers. She walked toward the car and leaned down to talk to him through the passenger window. "Are you sure you should be driving this soon? You were almost killed the other night, Professor Keaton. It just seems like after everything you've been through..."

He watched her fumble , his expression sober now. "I shouldn't be here at all, is that what you mean, Savannah? I shouldn't be alive when your friend is dead."

"No." She shook her head, embarrassed that he misunderstood her clumsy choice of words. "I didn't mean that. I would never think that."

"I tried to protect her. I tried to save her, Savannah." He heaved out a deep sigh. "There was nothing I could do. I hope you believe me. I hope you can forgive me."

"Of course," she murmured. "I'm sure you did everything you could. No one could blame you for what happened to Rachel."

As she spoke to reassure him, she couldn't keep the image of the monster's face from forming in her mind's eye. The horrible fangs. The fiery coals that were its eyes. Her skin went cold at the memory, sending a bone-deep shudder racing up her spine.

And yet Keaton seemed strangely unaffected. He seemed somehow removed from the terror of what he'd endured that night. Calmly accepting of the miracle of his survival following an attack by something inhuman, hellish. Either he truly didn't know the depth of the horror he endured, or he was hiding it from her.

Unless it was Savannah's gift that couldn't be trusted. It had never been fully in her control, but maybe it was becoming unreliable. Maybe she wasn't going crazy after all. Maybe she was simply losing her grasp of the ability she'd tried for so long to keep a secret from the rest of the world.

"I can't imagine how awful the experience must've been for you, Professor Keaton. You and Rachel both." She looked at him closely, searching for any cracks in his demeanor. "When you were trying to save her life, were you able to get a look at the attacker?"

"Yes," he replied, not so much as blinking. "I got a brief look, just before I was knocked unconscious."

Savannah's breath froze in her lungs. "Have you told anyone?"

"Of course. I told the police this morning, when they came to see me in the hospital as I was being discharged."

Savannah swallowed, not at all certain she wanted to hear her terror voiced by another person. "What did you tell them, Professor Keaton?"

"I told them what I saw. A vagrant who likely wandered in off the street, looking for something of value to pawn for his drug money. Rachel and I surprised him, and he attacked us like a wild animal."

Savannah listened, unable to speak for a moment. It didn't make sense. Not that what she saw in the glimpse from Rachel's bracelet made more sense, but she could tell Keaton was lying. "Are you sure about that? You're sure it was a vagrant, not...someone else?"

Keaton laughed then, a short bark of humor. He turned the radio off abruptly, his movements too quick. "Am I sure? I was the only one there to see what happened. Of course, I'm sure. What's this all about, Savannah? What's going on with you?"

"Nothing." She shook her head. "I'm just trying to understand what happened."

"I told you." He leaned farther across the cockpit of the Firebird, reaching for the door handle on the passenger side. "Where are you heading, anyway?"

"English Department," she replied woodenly, an inexplicable sense of unease spreading through her. "I have to meet with my professor about taking some coursework home with me on my leave of absence."

"You're leaving school?" He sounded surprised, but his face remained oddly unchanged, blank and unreadable. "Is it because of what happened?"

"I just need to go." She backed away from the door, careful to keep her steps subtle and her voice light as she hurried to formulate a protective lie. "There are some problems at home right now, and my family needs me there."

"I see." Keaton nodded. "I'm sure you've heard that Rachel's funeral is in Brookline later this week. I know you're all alone in Boston, so if you'd like, I could take you—"

"No, thank you." She had heard about the service, of course, and had already given her condolences and regrets to Rachel's mother when the distraught woman called to let her know the date and time of the gathering. "I'm leaving tonight for Louisiana. I've already got my bus ticket reserved and waiting for me."

"So soon," he remarked. "Well, then, at least let me give you a ride over to the English Department now. We can talk some more about all of this on the way."

Savannah's unease around him deepened. There was no way in hell she was getting near him the way he was acting. "I'm late as it is. It'll be faster if I cut across campus on foot." She forced a casual smile. "But thanks for offering, Professor Keaton. I really gotta go now."

"Suit yourself," he said, then turned the radio on again. "See you around, Savannah."

She gave him a bright nod as she retreated backward to the safety of the sidewalk and the hundreds of students still milling around on their lunch break. Savannah watched as Keaton drove away.

When he was out of sight, his white car disappearing around a corner onto another part of campus, she let out the breath she didn't realize she'd been holding. Then she pivoted in the opposite direction and ran like the devil was on her heels.

CHAPTER 9

Savannah sat on the edge of her hardside suitcase at the South Station bus terminal, her right knee bouncing with nervous energy. Her bus was late. She'd gone to the station a couple hours ahead of time that evening, eager to be on her way back home. Desperate, even.

Her troubling encounter with Professor Keaton had her rattled enough on top of everything else, but it was her phone call to the library after she'd gotten home to her apartment that had really compounded Savannah's state of confusion and mounting unease.

Mrs. Kennefick hadn't been able to help Savannah locate Gideon. Oh, she recalled the big blond man in black leather who'd come around the other night inquiring after Savannah.

"Hard not to notice a man like him," she'd said, understatement of the year. "He's not exactly the library's typical clientele."

No, there was nothing typical about Gideon at all. Except the fact that he was male, and apparently adept at lying to a woman's face. Because when she'd asked Mrs. Kennefick if she'd told Gideon where Savannah lived, the older woman had balked at the very idea.

"No, of course not, dear. One can never be too careful these days, sad to say. But he did tell me he was a friend of yours. I hope I didn't overstep when I informed him you'd called in sick."

Savannah had reassured her kindly old supervisor that she'd done nothing wrong, but inwardly she was awash in doubt about everything. Now she had to put Gideon in that number too. If Mrs. Kennefick hadn't sent him to Savannah's apartment, how had he found her? And why did he let her think he'd come across her address through honest means?

Nothing was making sense to her anymore. She couldn't help feeling suspicious of everything and everyone, as if her entire world was veering off the path of reality.

She needed a good dose of home to set her right, put her life back together. Help her put everything in its proper place again. She was eager for Amelie's good cooking, and her warm, soft shoulder to lean on.

If only the damn bus would get here.

Twenty minutes delayed now. Night had recently fallen outside the station. Evening rush hour commuters filled the place, hurrying to their trains and buses as exhaust fumes belched in through open doorways and garbled public address announcements squawked virtually unintelligibly from the ceiling speakers overhead.

No sooner had they come, the commuters were gone again, leaving Savannah and a few straggling others to wait a seemingly indeterminable time for some sign that they might actually make it out of the station tonight. She stood up on a deep yawn, just as the station speakers crackled to life and croaked out something indecipherable about the bus to Louisiana.

Savannah picked up her suitcase and hoofed it over to one of the counter attendants. "I missed the announcement just now. Did they say how long it will be before the bus to New Orleans begins boarding?"

"Ten minutes."

Finally. Just enough time to find a restroom and then she would be on her way at last. Savannah thanked the attendant, then headed off for the ladies' room farther up the terminal, luggage in hand. The bulky suitcase made for awkward walking. So awkward, that as she neared the bank of restrooms and payphones, she nearly tripped over the big, booted foot of a homeless person seated in the shadowy alcove just outside the ladies' room door.

"Excuse me," she murmured when she realized she'd bumped him.

He didn't seem to care. Or maybe he wasn't even aware of her at all, passed out or sleeping, she couldn't tell. The man in the tattered navy hoodie sweatshirt and filthy work pants didn't even lift his head. Savannah couldn't see his face. Long, dirty hair hung over his heavy brow and down past his chin.

Savannah attempted a better hold on her suitcase and skirted around his unmoving bulk to head into the restroom.

~ ~ ~

Gideon knew Savannah wasn't home, even before he knocked on her door. No lights on inside. No sound from within. No telltale glow through the walls as he searched for her with the gift of his sight.

"Shit."

Maybe he should have tried the library first, instead of checking for her at home. But even as he considered how quickly he could make it across town to look for her there, he was gripped with a sinking feeling of dread.

Savannah wouldn't have left Boston...would she?

That had been her intent last night, after all. He thought he might have convinced her to stay and let him help her, but what had he given her to hold on to? A heated kiss and a vague promise that he could somehow, miraculously, make everything better?

Fuck. He was an idiot to think she'd stick around on that flimsy incentive. He couldn't blame her if she finished packing her bag and took off for Louisiana as soon as he crept out of her bed twelve hours ago.

He couldn't have lost her so easily.

He *wouldn't* let her go so easily, damn it. And that claim had less to do with the Order's objectives or Darkhaven protocol than he cared to admit, even to himself.

If Savannah left, he was going after her.

Gideon took hold of the doorknob in death grip. Locked.

He was strong enough; he could have torn the damn thing off in his fist. But he was also Breed, and that meant he didn't have to resort to caveman tactics when he had more stealth tools at his command.

He mentally freed the two deadbolts from their tumblers. The door sprang open, and Gideon slipped inside the apartment. A quick scan of her bedroom told him his worst suspicions were correct.

Savannah's suitcase was gone. In the cramped little closet, a bunch of empty hangers.

"Damn it," he growled, stalking out to the living room where he'd kissed her just last night, held her in his arms while she slept against him on the sofa. He sent his gaze all over the place, looking for anything—a clue that might lead him to her.

He zeroed in on a memo pad lying next to the kitchen phone. He flashed across the room, more than walked, to pick up the note. In loopy, vibrant cursive handwriting, someone had jotted down *South Station,* followed by a number and a time. A bus schedule.

Savannah's departure for New Orleans.

She was leaving.

And if the schedule was accurate, she was already on her way.

Gone, more than twenty minutes ago.

Gideon flew out of there anyway, determined to catch her. He took off on foot, his Breed genetics carrying him much faster than any manmade vehicle could.

He was nothing but cold air on the humans he passed, his feet flying over pavement and through clogged traffic in the streets, speeding toward South Station.

~ ~ ~

Savannah parked her suitcase next to the paper towel dispenser in the empty restroom and stepped into the middle stall. She slid the wobbly lock into place, hearing the soft whoosh of the swinging entry door as someone came into the ladies' room a few seconds behind her. Hopefully someone who wouldn't think her battered American Tourister suitcase looked worthwhile to steal.

She was about to unzip her jeans, until the room echoed with the sudden sound of metal scraping heavily on concrete. As though someone were dragging the overflowing trash bin across the restroom floor. Was it the janitor coming in to clean?

"Hello? Someone's in here right now," she called out.

And then wished she'd kept her mouth shut because no one answered.

The room went very still, nothing but the soft trickle of water dripping into one of the clogged white sinks outside the stalls. Savannah froze, every animal instinct she had going taut with alarm.

She listened, hoping for the sound of someone's voice—an awkward apology for the intrusion, a request that she leave soon so the restroom could be maintained. She heard nothing. She was in there alone.

No, not alone.

There was a rasp of open-mouthed breathing from somewhere on the other side of the shaky metal door. Heavy boots scuffed on the filthy concrete floor. They stopped in front of her stall.

Savannah recognized them instantly.

It was the homeless man who'd been sleeping in the terminal outside.

A wash of fear swept over her, leaving her skin prickled with goosebumps, but she summoned the most threatening tone of voice she possessed. "You'd better get out of here right now, asshole, unless you want to spend the night in jail."

Through the soughing of his breath, a chuckle. Low and malicious. Not quite sane. Maybe not quite human.

Oh, God.

Savannah swallowed hard. She was trapped in the stall, didn't know whether to scream and bring someone else into her nightmare, or remain silent and pray that this was just another trick of her fracturing mind.

At least the threat was on the other side of the door. The metal panel wasn't the most sturdy, but it was locked from the inside. So long as she kept that door barred between them, she was safe.

But for how long?

She had her answer a second later.

While she stood there, trembling between the toilet and the door, the lock started to jiggle loose all on its own.

~ ~ ~

South Station was packed with passengers from a newly arrived train when Gideon skidded to a halt inside the terminal. Weaving between the sea of incoming humans, some striding with impatient purpose, others wandering aimlessly, Gideon searched out the schedule board and scanned the departures for Savannah's bus to New Orleans.

Delayed.

Which would have been excellent news, except the board was showing the bus had left the station. Departed just two minutes ago.

Gideon could hardly curb the need to put his fist through something. "Damn it."

He considered running after the bus. If he didn't catch up to it en route, odds were good that he'd find it at its first stop along the way. Then what? Hop on board and search Savannah out among the other passengers?

What would be the better tack once he found her: Trance her and carry her off the bus while attempting to avoid the notice of a few hundred witnesses? Or plop his ass into the seat next to her and give her a quick rundown on Breedmates, Rogues and other alien-spawned vampires right there on the Amtrak Number 59 to New Orleans?

Christ, what a disaster.

Not that he had a lot of choices here.

Gideon headed deeper into the terminal, mentally calculating potential outcomes of both less-than-ideal scenarios. As he stalked toward a corridor leading to the departure gates, he caught a whiff of something sickly sweet in the hallway.

Unmistakable to his Breed senses, the stench of a Rogue somewhere nearby.

Gideon glanced around, looking for the source of the odor. Nothing but humans in the station around him. Still, his nape prickled with certainty. His gaze slid to a yellow maintenance cone blocking the door to the ladies' room across the hall. He strode closer, and the foul scent of a feral vampire strengthened.

His talent penetrated the wood and steel swinging door, locking on to a pair of heat sources inside. One was massive and hulking. The other, tall and slender, frozen in place before the threat facing her.

Ah, fuck.

Savannah.

Gideon's entire body ignited in hot, ferocious rage. One second he was in the terminal hallway, the next he was in the closed public restroom, shoving past the overturned rubbish can and leaping on the Rogue—just as the suckhead was about to crowd into the stall to attack Savannah.

On a low growl, Gideon heaved the vampire away from Savannah. He drove the Rogue's spine into the wall of white sinks and dirty mirrors on the opposite side of the room. On impact, one of the old basins crashed to the floor, shattering on a heavy thump at Gideon's feet. Water sprayed from the broken spigot, hissing almost as fiercely as the feral vampire struggling to free itself of Gideon's unyielding hold.

The suckhead grunted and snarled, gnashing its yellowed fangs. It reeked of Bloodlust and the soured evidence of a recent feeding, but its amber eyes and thin, slitted pupils held the look of a ravenous beast still thirsting for blood.

That this beast had gotten so close to Savannah—mere seconds away from touching her, biting her, close enough to kill her—made Gideon's veins throb with the need to punish.

To eviscerate the son of a bitch who intended her harm.

And he would have, had Savannah not been in the room to witness it.

Her stricken face was reflected in the cracked glass of the mirror behind the Rogue's struggling bulk. Savannah's dark doe eyes were wide with terror, her pretty mouth dropped open in a silent scream as she stared at Gideon and the beast pinned between him and the restroom wall.

"Get out of here," Gideon told her, ready to end the suckhead and loath to do it in front of her. "Wait for me outside, Savannah. You don't want to see this."

But she didn't move. Maybe she couldn't. Or maybe it was the sheer tenacity of the woman, her sharp, curious mind, that would not give in to fright when the need for answers was stronger.

The Rogue bucked and thrashed, trying to throw Gideon off. There was little time to hesitate. The din of the terminal outside the restroom door would mask most of the sounds of struggle, but he had to end this quickly, before they drew unwanted attention. Gideon pulled one of his long daggers from the sheath beneath his black trench coat.

The suckhead's amber eyes rolled toward the movement. Awareness of his impending death flashed across the open-mawed sneer. He roared, one filthy hand shooting out to the side of him, grabbing for some kind of weapon of his own.

He didn't get the chance.

Gideon shifted his hold and brought his dagger up between their bodies. With a hard thrust, the blade sank deep, plunging into the center of the Rogue's chest. The suckhead froze, panting rapidly, the twin coals of his eyes fixed on Gideon, hideous face sagging in defeat.

Gideon held the dagger in place as the diseased Breed vampire shuddered around the killing length of titanium-edged steel.

Death was immediate. Gideon dropped the big corpse as the titanium began to feed on the Rogue, dissolving it from the inside out. In mere minutes, the lump of dying flesh and bone would be nothing more than ash, then all evidence of its existence gone altogether.

Gideon turned to face Savannah. "Are you hurt?"

Mutely, she shook her head. "Gideon...who was he? What was he?" She drew in a ragged breath. "My God, what the hell is going on?"

Gideon stowed his bloodied blade and went to her. He pulled her trembling body under his arm and gently lifted her face. "Did he touch you?"

"No," she murmured. "But if you hadn't been here..."

He kissed her, a brief, tender brush of his mouth against hers. "I'm here. I will keep you safe, Savannah. Do you trust me?"

"Yes," she whispered. "I trust you." She peered around him, to where the dead Rogue was swiftly disintegrating, clothing and all. "But I don't understand any of this. How can any of this be real?"

"Come on." He took her hand in his. "There could be more where that one came from. We have to go now."

He led her out of the restroom, back into the bustle of the station. It wasn't until they were standing at the curb in the cool night air that Gideon realized he was at a loss as to where to go.

Savannah's apartment was across town, several miles away. Not that it seemed like a smart idea to take her there. He doubted very much that the Rogue going after her at the bus station was a random thing. Whoever put the suckhead on her trail would no doubt have her apartment under watch too. And as much as Gideon wanted to know who that someone was, Savannah's wellbeing was his sole concern now.

Which should have been cause enough to send him with her to the nearest Darkhaven.

To be sure, that would be the most logical, pragmatic choice. But logic and pragmatism could get fucked right about now, for all he cared about that.

He wasn't ready to yank Savannah away from harrowing situation and a thousand questions in need of answers, only to turn her over to the diplomatic arm of the Breed nation. In fact, he was finding it hard to imagine a scenario where he'd ever be ready to hand her over to someone else and walk away. He felt her soft fingers tighten around his broad palm as she stood beside him in the dark, waiting for him to make his choice.

Trusting him to keep her safe, as he promised he would.

Gideon glanced into her velvet brown gaze and knew a sudden, fierce protectiveness surge through him. Sending her away now was out of the question. It was his duty to walk her into his world gently. He bristled at the thought of letting some stranger out of the Enforcement Agency or civilian ranks step in where this woman was concerned.

His woman.

The claim swept up on him from somewhere deep in his subconscious, a sharp, primal thing. It throbbed in his veins, drumming hard in his ears with every beat of his heart.

And he needed her too.

After seeing her so close to danger back in the station—after realizing how quickly he might have lost her tonight—Gideon wanted nothing more than pull Savannah against him and never let her out of his sight again.

He wasn't going to push her off on the Darkhavens or the Enforcement Agency, even if that meant willfully ignoring Breed protocol.

Even if that meant blatantly defying Lucan's orders.

Gideon reached into the pocket of his black fatigues and withdrew the scrap of paper Tegan had given him back the compound earlier that day. He read it for a second time. Just an address, nothing more.

An address that was only a few blocks away from where he stood now.

He wasn't sure what to expect when they got there, but at the moment it seemed to be his best and only option.

"Let's go," he murmured, brushing his mouth against the warmth of her temple.

And with Savannah tucked under the shelter of his arm, clinging to him like a life line, Gideon guided her away from the busy bus terminal.

CHAPTER 10

WHAT is this place?"

Savannah stood beside Gideon on a quiet, historic residential street little more than a mile from South Station, by her guess. Before them loomed a slim, three-story redbrick townhouse. It was stately, but unremarkably so next to its handsome, welcoming neighbors.

No lights glowed from within this house, no sounds emanated from within its walls. Its windows were dark, shuttered tight with black slatted panels. The iron-and-glass porch light was cold, leaving the walkway and stoop unlit as she and Gideon had made their way up to the heavy wood door.

The house, for all its seemingly deliberate effort to blend in with the others on the street, stood forbidding in its utter stillness.

Savannah rubbed off the chill that raced up her arms as she took in the stoic slab of brick and darkness. "Does anyone live here? It's as quiet as a tomb."

"I've never been here before," Gideon said. Head down, he stared with steady intent on the deadbolt drilled into the thick oak door. Although she didn't notice if he had a key, in mere seconds, the lock was freed and Gideon opened the door for her. "Come inside."

She followed him, pausing in the unfamiliar place, uncertain. Still shaken from what happened at the bus station. "It's so dark in here."

"Stay where you are." His deep voice with its soothing accent was a low rumble beside her, his blunt fingertips warm where he stroked the side of her face. "I'll find you some light."

She waited while he ably crossed the room and turned on a small lamp several feet away from her.

The soft illumination revealed a nearly vacant living space. One lone chair—a rough-hewn relic from the turn of the previous century, at least—sat beside the simple wooden table where the lamp now glowed. On the other side of the room, the cold, black mouth of a fireplace seemingly long out of use laced the stale air with the acrid tinge of old wood smoke.

Savannah cautiously trailed Gideon as he left the main living area to enter an adjacent room. She crossed her arms in front of her, tucking her bare fingers in to her sides to avoid the inadvertent touch that would wake her extrasensory ability. She suspected this house had never been filled with family or laughter. She didn't need to rouse her gift and confirm it.

No, she'd had enough darkness to last her a good long while.

"We'll be safe here, Savannah." Gideon turned on another lamp in the space where he stood now. He removed his black leather trench coat and laid it on the bed. Fastened around the hips of his black combat fatigues, he wore a thick belt studded with all manner of weapons—a pair of pistols, an array of knives, including the savage blade that he'd wielded back at the station. He took off the belt and placed it on top of his coat. "Savannah, I give you my word, I'm not going to let anything happen to you. You know you can trust me on that, yeah?"

She nodded and stepped into the modest bedroom, noting immediately the lack of decoration or personal effects. The bed was made, but fitted in plain sheets and a single pillow.

The kind of bed one might expect to see in a soldier's barracks, more so than a home.

There was a sadness in this place.

A deep, mournful sorrow.

And rage.

Black, raw...consuming.

Savannah shuddered under the weight of it. But it was the memory of what she witnessed earlier that night that threatened to take her legs out from under her.

"Gideon, what happened back there?" God, just speaking of it now made her head reel all over again. She had so many questions. They spilled out of her in a rush. "How did you know to look for me? How could you have known where I was—that I was in trouble behind that closed door of the restroom? How were you able to do what you did to that...that *monster?* I saw what happened. You stabbed him, and he—" She exhaled a shaky breath, wanting to deny what she witnessed, yet certain it was real. "You stabbed him and he disintegrated. You killed him as if it was no big thing. As if you'd seen that kind of monster a hundred times before."

"More times than that, Savannah." Gideon strode over to her, his handsome face sober, alarmingly so. "I've killed hundreds like him."

"Hundreds," she murmured, swallowing past the staggering word. "Gideon, that man...that creature...it wasn't human."

"No."

Savannah stared at him, struggling to process his calm reply. She had hoped he'd offer some kind of logical explanation for what was going on, some kind of reasonable denial that would soothe the panic rising inside her.

But the quick wit and reassuring confidence that usually glinted in his blue eyes was nowhere to be found. His expression was filled with a quiet gravity that made him seem both tender and lethal at the same time. Two qualities she had seen firsthand in him during the short time she'd known him.

She drew in breath, tried to tamp down the hysteria that threatened to climb up her throat and choke off her air. "That same kind of monster killed Rachel. And those little boys I saw when I touched that old sword in the Art History collection—they were slaughtered by a group of that same kind of monster. I tried to tell you that when you came to check in on me at my apartment last night. I didn't want to believe it then. I still don't."

"I know." He reached out and gently smoothed his hand along her cheek. "And as I told you last night, I'm here for you, Savannah. I want to help you make sense of it all."

She stared up into his gaze. "Vampires," she said quietly, her voice threadbare, fear still raw and ripe in her breast. "That's what we're talking about, isn't it. That man at the bus terminal. The ones I saw when I touched the sword and Rachel's bracelet...they were vampires."

Something flickered in his gaze now. There was an uncharacteristic hesitation in his steady voice. "By the most basic definition, yes. That's what they were."

"Oh, my God." It had been hard enough to come to grips with the idea when it only lived in her head. But to hear him speak it now—to have witnessed Gideon gutting one of the creatures right in front of her—made the reality crash down on her like a suffocating wave. "You're telling me vampires are real. They're real, and you somehow know how to kill them."

"I, along with a few others like me, yes." He was studying her now, measuring her in some way, as if he wasn't sure she could handle his answers. "Not all of the Breed are like the one who came after you at the station. Or the one who killed your friend. Or the ones who murdered those innocent boys. Only Rogues do that, Savannah. The most depraved, diseased individuals."

"This is madness, Gideon. I don't want to hear any more right now. I can't."

"Savannah, you need to understand that there are dangers in this world. Dangers that few people truly comprehend. After tonight—after everything you've seen—you can't go back to your old life. Maybe not ever. You're part of something darker now, and there are things you need to know if you're going to survive—"

"No." She shook her head and drew away from Gideon's soothing touch. Everything was happening too fast. She was confused and shaken, too overwhelmed to process anything more. "I've heard enough for now. I don't want to hear any more about monsters or danger or death. I'm trying to hold it together, Gideon, but I'm just so fucking scared."

She put her face in her palms, struggling not to lose it in front of him, but failing miserably. A sob shook her. Then Gideon's arm wrapped around her and drew her up against his strong, warm body. He didn't say anything, simply held her close and let her regain herself for a moment.

"I'm so confused," she murmured against his chest. "I'm terrified."

"Don't be." He caressed her back, his touch a welcome comfort, easing her anxiety. His body felt so powerful around her, solid and sheltering, engulfing her in his steady strength. "The last thing I want is for you to be confused," he whispered against her temple. "I don't want you to be afraid of anything. Least of all me."

"Afraid of you? No." She gave a slow shake of her head, then pressed her brow to the center of his chest, feeling the hard drum of his heartbeat against her. "You're the only thing that feels real to me, Gideon. Of everything that's happened the past few days, the only thing I know for sure right now is the way you make me feel."

His answering growl was low, vibrating from somewhere deep inside him. She felt his muscles twitch as he continued to hold her, his strength coiled and deadly, yet wrapped around her with utmost tenderness.

Savannah lifted her head to meet his gaze. His eyes had gone darker in the dim lamplight, yet in the depths of all that stormy blue, a mesmerizing fire seemed to crackle. The heat in him was a palpable thing, radiating into her everywhere they touched.

"You felt right to me last night, Gideon, when you kissed me. I was scared then too, but you felt so right." She reached up to catch his rigid jaw in the cradle of her hand. "How is it you came into my life just when I needed you most?"

He said her name, a thick whisper that leaked from between his clenched teeth. A torment seemed to sweep over him, every sinew growing taut and still as they stood together in the meager sanctuary of the bedroom.

"If anything scares me when it comes to you," she confided softly, "it's how much I need to feel your arms around me like this. You make me feel safe, Gideon. In a way I never knew before. You make me feel as though nothing bad can touch me so long as I'm with you."

"It can't. I won't allow that. Not so long as I am breathing." His voice was thunder, deep and rumbling. "You'll always be safe, Savannah. I'll stake my life on that."

She smiled, moved by the ferocity of his vow. "Spoken like one of Arthur's noble knights. I've never had my own hero."

He blew out a low, strangled curse. "No, not noble. And most certainly not anyone's hero. Just someone who cares about you. A man who wants to know you're never in harm's way. A man who wants you to find the happiness you deserve. A man who wants...ah, fuck." His gaze burned as he looked at her. "I'm a man who wants too damn much where you're concerned.."

Savannah watched the tension play across his lean, angular cheeks and the broad line of his mouth. It deepened when his hot gaze locked on to her unflinching stare. "What do you want, Gideon?"

His searing eyes drank her in, and when he spoke, his answer came in the form of a guttural, almost animal snarl. "I want this," he said, and brought her deeper into his embrace with only the faintest twitch of the muscles that held her caged against him. Power coursed through him with barely an effort, his pulse points drumming against her skin everywhere their bodies connected.

"And this." He softly skated his fingertips along the side of her face, then brushed the pad of his thumb across her lower lip. Lowering his head to hers, he descended on her until their mouths were less than a breath apart. "And I want this."

He kissed her.

Not the slow meeting of their lips from the other night, but a hungered kiss that claimed her mouth without apology, his tongue pushing past her teeth in fevered demand. He growled something indiscernible as he crushed her against him, his breath coming fast and hard, hot against her face.

His mouth consumed her. Drank her in with a ferocity that both startled and enflamed her.

Gideon's hold on her tightened. His arousal was unmistakable, a hard, heavy presence that called to the most primal part of her. Savannah's body answered, pooling with warm need at her core. She moaned as Gideon's kiss deepened, passion-filled, questing. So naked with desire, it sucked the breath from her lungs.

He dragged her body flush against him now, catching her nape in his big hand. His fingers burned where they wrapped around the side of her neck, branding his touch on her skin.

And his kiss owned her too.

Her pulse throbbed everywhere he touched her, building to a roar that filled her ears as his lips and tongue consumed her. She gave it back to him, meeting his tongue with hers and drawing him deep. Pleasure rumbled through him, low like thunder, vibrating against her breasts and belly.

Savannah arced into him as his free hand found the hem of her sweater and slipped inside. His hard, hot fingers ran up her ribs and over the thin lace of her bra. She groaned with pleasure, lost to his touch as he kneaded her breasts and continued to wreak havoc on her senses with his kiss.

"I have to have you, Savannah," he rasped against her lips, breathless, his voice oddly thick. "Ah, Christ...I've never wanted anything more than I want this with you now. I want *you*. All of you."

He didn't wait for permission. Stripping off her sweater and bra and tossing them aside, he bent to lavish her bare breasts with the delicious heat of his mouth. Her nipples were taut and achy under his attention, the wet need in her core turning to fiery lava with every lap and nip and suckle of his mouth.

Desperate to have her hands on him, she reached down to the zippered fly of his black fatigues and felt the steely bulge of his cock swell even fuller under her palm and fingers. His sex was raw power beneath her hand, pulsing with carnal demand.

She was on fire for him too. Hungry with the same need, the same urgency to feel his hard body up against her, inside her. She gripped him through the fabric, and he tore away from her breasts on a ragged growl. Head down, he kissed a descending trail of fire across her ribs and abdomen, sinking to his haunches before her. His questing mouth went lower then, teasing her sensitive skin above the low-slung waistline of her hip-hugging jeans.

"Gideon, yes," she panted, trembling with sensation, her own words little more than a gasp of sound. "Oh, God, yes. I need this too. I need you now."

She sucked in a shallow gasp as he unfastened the buttons and tugged both jeans and panties down with one swift, unswerving motion. Cool air hit the naked tops of her thighs and the exposed thatch of curls between them. Then a moment later, it was all heat, as Gideon pressed his face to her mound and kissed that most private place.

Savannah dropped her hands to his shoulders, holding on for dear life as his mouth closed down on her sex. His tongue cleaved into the seam of her, wet and hot and wicked. He suckled her, taking her tight little pearl between his teeth, toying with it, swirling the tip of his tongue over her flesh and making her mewl with mounting pleasure.

"You taste so sweet, Savannah," he told her between those erotic, sensual kisses. "I wanna eat you up. Lick every sweet inch of you. Hear you scream my name."

Oh, God, it wouldn't take much more, she thought, closing her eyes and dropping her head back on her shoulders as he gripped her bare ass and buried his face between her parted legs. He teased her clit with his mouth, tantalizing strokes as he gently spread the swollen, wet petals of her core with fingertips made slick from her body's juices.

"So tight," he murmured, penetrating her slowly with just one finger. Her body clung to him instantly, greedily, her thighs quivering as he lapped at her and worked his finger inside the core of her sex. "God, Savannah...I knew you were extraordinary, but damn. I never would've been ready for this. You're so sweet the way you respond to me. So fucking beautiful."

She moaned at his sensual praise, the only reply she could manage as her blood rushed feverishly through her veins, setting every nerve ending on fire.

And Gideon gave her no quarter whatsoever. His fingers played her with masterful skill. His mouth was relentless, his tongue so very, very good.

Her legs were going boneless beneath her. She clutched his head, buried her fingers in the short blond silk of his hair as her pleasure built and crested, about to crash into her. "Gideon," she gasped. "I can't take anymore. Please...you have to stop..."

"Never," he growled. "Let go, baby. Let me take you there."

Her knees were jelly, the muscles of her thighs quaking as the rush of orgasm roared up on her.

"Mmm, that's it, Savannah," he coaxed. "Come for me. Let me hear you."

Her voice was a strangled cry as he suckled her harder, driving her higher as her climax raced for its peak. She couldn't slow it down. Couldn't hold it back another moment.

And then she did scream his name. It tore out of her on a ragged gasp as her entire being shattered against Gideon's mouth. She was still quivering with aftershocks as he rose up from his crouch and quickly shed his pants.

"Shirt too," she murmured, drowning in pleasure but wanting to feel his naked skin against her. He hesitated for a moment, his face averted—a strange pause that might have registered more fully, had she not been wrapped in the fog of the most incredible orgasm she'd ever had.

Gideon pulled off his shirt and she caught only a fleeting glimpse of intricate, tribal-like tattoos on his chest in the instant before he swooped down on her with a fevered kiss. "I need to be inside you," he growled, sounding dark and hungered, the rough scrape of his deep voice virtually unrecognizable. "Now, Savannah."

"Yes," she agreed, needing to feel more of him too. "Now."

He claimed her with a kiss so savage and carnal, it rocked her. She felt herself moving backward swiftly, her feet hardly touching the floor. She came up hard against the wall of the bedroom, Gideon's big body covering her. His mouth still locked on hers, his strong hands drifted down to cup the cheeks of her ass. He squeezed her possessively, his erection rising hot and proud against her hip. He shifted his weight on his feet, catching her in a different hold now. Then he lifted her as though she weighed no more than a feather, guiding her legs around him.

He felt so good against her, warm and hard and hungry.

So real.

In the midst of so much terror and confusion, being with Gideon was the only place she felt safe.

She'd never known anything that felt so right.

"Take me now," she murmured. "Take all that you want, Gideon."

He didn't answer. Not in words, that is.

Holding her aloft in his hands, he thrust his pelvis forward and seated her to the hilt on the thick spear of his cock. He moved with urgent strokes, in and out, deeper and then deeper still, pistoning her on his length.

Savannah felt tension rack him as his tempo increased to a fevered pitch. His shoulders were granite under her curled fingers, his muscles bunched and knotted as she clung to him and let him chase his own climax.

He found it swiftly, his hips bucking wildly, pushing farther inside with every claiming pound of his flesh against hers. Savannah was already breaking apart again, splintering with pleasure, as Gideon roared a wordless, reverent-sounding oath and filled her with the hot rush of his release.

CHAPTER 11

Bill Keaton knew he had company at his house in Southie that night, even before the tall, impeccably suited man peeled away from the shadows inside the front door.

He'd been expecting this visit, forbidden to ever seek the man out, but to wait always for his instructions. To carry them out without question or failure. Keaton was loath to disappoint, and he knew the news he had to impart tonight would not be welcome.

He got up from his recliner and left his half-baked frozen dinner sitting untouched on the TV tray to greet his visitor. Behind him in the living room, the television blared with sirens and gunshot sound effects. One of those cop dramas he watched every week, but now couldn't recall why. Like the salisbury steak and mashed potatoes he'd warmed up for dinner more than an hour ago, he found he no longer had the taste for any of the things he once enjoyed.

He was different since the incident at the university a few nights ago.

He was a changed man.

And the cause of that change now stood before him in expectant silence inside Keaton's house. Keaton gave a deferential nod of greeting, as respectful as a bow.

"Did the individual sent to deal with the girl show up as planned tonight?"

"Yes," Keaton replied, eyes remaining downcast, subservient. "Everything was in place, just as we discussed."

"So, the girl is dead?"

"She is not," Keaton answered, anxious now. He hazarded to lift his eyes and meet the hard stare of the one he served. "She lives. I saw her leave the station with a man."

The shrewd gaze narrowed on him, sparking with deadly fire. "What man?"

"Big," Keaton said. "Tall. A blond thug in a black leather trench coat. I saw weaponry belted at his waist, but he was no police officer or law enforcer. And he was not mortal."

This Keaton understood with full certainty, just one of the new senses he'd acquired a few nights ago, when his eyes were opened to a dark, hidden new world. The world this man showed him when he made Keaton all over again.

"Did they see you—the girl and her companion?"

Keaton gave a slow shake of his head. "No. I realized what he was, and so I made sure not to be noticed. He is one of your kind."

A grunt of acknowledgment, while the fire in those predator's eyes crackled even more coldly. "Of course, he is one of my kind. All the worse, he's one of the Order." Then, more to himself, he mused, "Could he possibly know about me? Does he realize I have that sword, after all this time?"

The sharp gaze came back to Keaton now. "You saw them leave the station together. Where did they go?"

"I don't know," Keaton answered, supposing that he should feel fear to admit that, yet compelled only to speak the truth to the one who owned him now. "I saw the girl and her companion exit the terminal, but then they vanished. I don't know where they've gone. I went to her apartment in Allston to wait, but they never arrived there."

A growl erupted from between gritted teeth. "I need to find that girl before she tells the Order what she knows. Fuck, it may be too late for that already."

"Shall I locate the individual we sent to the station tonight and have him stake out her apartment?" Keaton offered, eager to provide a solution.

His suggestion earned only a dismissive wave. "That particular weapon is of no use now. Gideon will have killed the Rogue for certain. Then again, maybe this setback can work to my advantage." A dark smile broke over his ageless, unlined face. "To think, I nearly killed my Breedmate when she stupidly gave away a number of my private mementos to the university. She didn't know, of course. She couldn't know. I never told her about that sword or how I came to have it."

"And now you have it in your possession again," Keaton said. "I am pleased to have served you in retrieving what belongs to you."

The answering bark of laughter was sharp-edged, humorless. "As I recall," he muttered, "I gave you no choice, Keaton. Once you saw what I did to that slut you were fucking in your office, you broke easily enough."

Keaton felt no reaction to the reminder of his cowardice. He was detached from the whole event, freed of all the weaknesses of his former self. All that mattered to him now was doing what was needed, what his Master commanded of him.

"I will see to it that the task is carried out as you wish, Sire. Savannah Dupree will die."

"No. I think not." The vampire who owned Keaton's life and mind now—his soul itself—paused with unrushed deliberation. "I have a better plan. Find her. Bring her to me. Since she obviously is of some interest to the warrior, Gideon, she can help me finish a score he started centuries ago."

~ ~ ~

Take all that you want.

Savannah's tender offer pounded in Gideon's temples—in his blood—hours after they'd made love. He'd left her satiated and softly sleeping in the bedroom a short while ago, while he slipped out to the main room of the empty old house to work off some of his restless energy.

Shirtless, dressed only in his black fatigues, he went through a series of quick, sweeping combat maneuvers with the long dagger from his weapons belt. He kept his hands and body in much-needed motion. His mind churned on vivid recollections of the passion he'd shared with Savannah, earth-shaking passion that still had his veins lit up and electric. Other parts of his anatomy were running on a short leash too.

But undercurrent of the incredible pleasure he'd taken from Savannah was the guilt he felt for having hidden himself—his true self—from her, even while she had surrendered everything she had to him.

Take all that you want, Gideon.

"Fuck," he muttered, low beneath his breath. If she only knew how much he wanted.

He pivoted on his bare heel to make a savage swipe at an invisible opponent. Himself, or the Rogue who accosted Savannah tonight? He wasn't sure who was the bigger villain tonight.

He needed to tell her what he was. It would have to be Savannah's choice how she chose to think of him, after he gave her the truth she rightfully deserved a few hours ago.

The truth she deserved from the moment he first realized the pretty, innocent young student was a Breedmate, not a simple *Homo sapiens* female. Savannah deserved a hell of a lot more than he'd given her so far.

And if he was being honest with himself, she deserved more than he could ever hope to offer her as the mate of a male whose past was steeped in bloodshed and failure. A warrior whose future was pledged in full to the Order.

He needed to explain all of that and more to Savannah. Damn it, he'd meant to before things had gotten so far out of hand tonight. He'd let himself get too entangled, and now he was caught in a trap of his own making.

It would take time and some doing to make things right now. Time alone with Savannah being a luxury he didn't expect he'd have for much longer.

After what happened at the bus terminal, it was imperative that Savannah be given the full protection and sanctuary the Breed nation had to offer. Before the danger that pursued her came any closer than it had earlier tonight.

As much as Gideon wanted to deny it, it was no coincidence that the Rogue just happened to go after Savannah at the station. He had stalked her there. Not through blood thirst or basic opportunity. Gideon would bet his sword arm that someone had sent the suckhead after her.

More than likely, the same someone who had killed her roommate and left her professor for dead. The same someone who was now, apparently, in possession of the sword used to slaughter Gideon's kin.

He needed to find the bastard and bring him down.

Before Savannah ended up any further into the crossfire.

They couldn't stay here forever. Wherever they were. Tegan had never mentioned this place before. Even though the warrior had offered the old house up to Gideon, he had no misconceptions that Tegan meant it to be a very temporary shelter. Frankly, Gideon had to agree with Savannah that the place felt more like a neglected tomb than a home.

As much as Gideon hated to admit it, she needed to be moved to a more suitable, more permanent, arrangement. And unless he had lost his mind and meant to defy Lucan Thorne's edict for a second time in so many days, he couldn't very well bring Savannah to the compound. Gideon could just imagine how the Order's unyielding Gen One leader would react to a civilian being brought there against long-standing Order protocol.

But if she went there as Gideon's mate?

The notion hit him hard. Not because it was a fucking crazy, bad idea. But because of how sane and right it felt to him.

Savannah at his side, bonded together in blood and life for somewhere close to forever.

Take all that you want, Gideon.

Savannah, his Breedmate.

Holy hell . . . .

The thought opened up something hot and deep in his chest. A longing. A yearning so total, it rendered him motionless, unbreathing.

Ah, Christ.

The bloody last thing he needed was to let himself fall in love with Savannah.

He cursed roundly, making a vicious stab at the air with the long dagger he'd used to gut the Rogue who'd gone after Savannah. Pivoting on his bare heel, he lunged into another mock strike, this one intended for the unknown enemy he was determined to unmask—right before he would force that Breed male to swallow the same steel that killed his Rogue errand boy.

It was at that moment Gideon heard a soft stirring in the other room.

Savannah was out of bed. She drifted into the open doorway of the adjacent room where he stood, the long dagger gripped in his hand, his motion suspended in the stance of a man poised to kill.

"Savannah."

She stared at him, her big brown eyes still drowsy, her beautiful, lithe body utterly naked. So stunning.

Gideon drank in the sight of her with a greedy gaze, his pulse kicking with swift, fierce arousal.

But she wasn't looking at him the same way.

She seemed stricken somehow. Wooden with silent shock.

"Oh, my God," she murmured after a moment. Her voice was small and breathless, though not from sleep or desire. She gaped at him in a mix of shock and hurt, her pretty face twisted with confusion. "Oh, my God...I knew you looked familiar. I knew I'd seen you somewhere before—"

"Savannah, what's wrong?" He set the blade down on the fireplace mantel and headed toward her.

"No." She shook her head, held out a hand as if to bar him from getting any closer. "I saw you before, Gideon. When I held the old sword, I saw the murder of those two little boys all those years ago...but I also saw you."

His blood ran cold in the face of her fear. "Savannah—"

"I saw you, like this, with a blade in your hand—the way you looked just now," she said, talking over him. "Except it wasn't you. It couldn't be you."

He didn't speak, couldn't refute what she was saying. What she saw with her Breedmate's gift.

"I mean, how could it be you, right?" she pressed, a raw edge to her words. "The man I saw should be a couple of centuries dead by now."

"I can explain," he offered lamely.

He stepped closer toward her, but she flinched away. She crossed her arms over herself as if she were naked in front of a stranger now. "You're not human," she murmured. "You can't be."

He cursed softly. "I don't want you to be afraid of me, Savannah. If you would just hear me out now—"

"Oh, God." She barked out a sharp laugh. "You're not even going to try to deny it?"

He felt a tendon tick heavily in his jaw. "I wanted to explain everything to you, but not while you were upset. You said yourself tonight you weren't ready to hear more."

She staggered back a pace, shaking her head in mute denial. Her stare had gone distant, turning inward. He was losing her. She was pulling away from him as something to be mistrusted, feared. Maybe even reviled. "I have to get out of here," she murmured flatly. "I have to go home. I have to call my sister. She was expecting me to be on the bus tonight, and I..."

She broke away then, turning to rush back into the bedroom. She made a frantic circuit of the room, started retrieving her clothing.

Gideon followed her. "Savannah, you can't run away from this. You're in too deep now. We both are."

She didn't respond. She grabbed her panties off the floor and hastily stepped into them, flashing the dark thatch of silk between her legs and giving him an intimate glimpse of her long, satiny thighs and creamy mocha skin.

Skin he'd tasted everywhere and longed to savor again.

Without speaking to him or looking at him, she searched for her bra. Her small breasts swayed with her movements as she shrugged into the little scrap of lace.

Arousal stirred inside Gideon, too powerful for him to hold back. He couldn't curb his swift physical reaction to the sight of her, so pretty and disheveled from his lovemaking of a few hours ago. His *glyphs* started to churn to life on his skin. His gums tingled with the awakening of his fangs.

Hastily, she grabbed up her sweater and jeans, holding them to her as she rushed past him, head-down, out of the bedroom.

He followed swiftly, stalking behind her.

"Savannah, you can't leave. I can't let you go home now. It's too late." His voice was gravel, roughened by his rising desire and the fierce need to make her understand the full truth now.

He flashed over to where she stood, faster than she could possibly track him. He put his hand on her shoulder where the small scarlet teardrop-and-crescent-moon Breedmate mark stamped her flawless skin. "Damn it, stop shutting me out. Listen to me."

She whirled around, her eyes wide. His own gaze felt hot in his skull, must have blazed back at her in that moment as bright as lit coals. By some miracle of deception and desperate will, he'd been able to conceal his transformation from her earlier tonight, but not now. Nor did he try.

"Oh, my God," she moaned, fear bleeding into her voice. She struggled in his hold, turned her head askance on a strangled gasp of horror.

Gideon took her chin and gently guided her face back toward his. "Savannah, look at me. See me. Trust me. You said you did."

Her eyes fell slowly to his open mouth and the tips of his fangs, which stretched longer every second. After a long moment, she looked back up into his fiery stare. "You're one of them. You're a monster, just like them. A Rogue—"

"No," he denied firmly. "Not Rogue, Savannah. But I am Breed, like they are. Like they were, before they lost themselves to Bloodlust."

"A vampire," she clarified, maybe needing to say the word out loud. Her voice dropped to something less than a whisper. "Are you undead?"

"No." He resisted the urge to laugh off the crude misconception as ridiculous, but only because she was so obviously horrified at the thought. "I'm not undead, Savannah. That's where myth and reality differ the most when it comes to my kind. The Breed is otherworldly in origin. Big difference."

She gaped at him now, studying him. He didn't mind her blatant inspection, since the longer he stood still before her, the calmer she seemed to become. "You have nothing to fear from me," he told her, speaking the words as a promise. A solemn vow. "You need never fear me, Savannah.."

She swallowed hard, her gaze flicking over every inch of his face, his mouth, his *dermaglyph*-covered chest and shoulders.

When she hesitantly lifted her hand then dropped it back to her side again, Gideon took her fingers in a loose grasp and gently brought her palm to his mouth. He kissed its warm center, giving her none of his sharp edges, only the soft, warm heat of his mouth. Then he guided her hand to his chest, resting it over the heavy beat of his heart. "Feel me,

Savannah. I'm flesh and blood and bone, just like you. And I will never harm you."

She kept her hand there, even after he let go. "Tell me how any of this is possible," she murmured. "How can any of this be real?"

Gideon smoothed his fingers along her cheek, then down along the pulse point of her carotid, that fluttered like a caged bird against the pad of his thumb. "Get dressed first," he instructed her tenderly, more for his own good than hers. "Then sit down and we'll talk."

She glanced over at the lone wooden chair in the living room of Tegan's desolate house. To Gideon's relief, she looked back at him not in terror or revulsion, but with the arch wisdom and keen wit of a woman better than twice her young age. "Time for me to risk my own Seat Perilous?"

"I doubt there's ever been anyone more worthy," he replied.

And if he wasn't already half in love with her, Gideon reckoned he fell a little harder in that moment.

CHAPTER 12

Gideon had paced in front of her the entire time he spoke.

Now that he had finished, he finally paused, watching her with an expectant, oddly endearing kind of silence as Savannah worked to absorb everything she'd just heard.

"Are you all right?" he asked carefully, when the weight of her new education rendered her speechless. "Still with me, Savannah?"

She nodded, trying to make all the pieces fit together in her mind.

The whole incredible history of his kind and where they came from, how they lived in secret alongside humans for thousands of years. And how Gideon and a small number of like-minded, courageous Breed males—modern-day, dark knights, from the sound of it—worked together as a unit right there in Boston to keep the city safe from the violence of Rogues.

It was all pretty mind-boggling.

But she believed him.

She trusted him at his word that the fantastical tale he'd just told her was the truth.

It was, whether she was prepared to accept it or not, her new reality.

A reality that seemed a little less terrifying having Gideon in it with her.

She glanced up at him. "Vampires from outer space, huh?"

He smiled wryly. "The Ancients were otherworlders, not little green men. Deadly predators unlike this planet has ever seen. The very top of the food chain."

"Right. But their offspring—"

"The Breed."

"The Breed," she said, still testing everything out in her mind. "They're part human?"

"Hybrid progeny of the Ancients and Breedmates, females like you," he clarified.

Savannah reached up to her left shoulder blade, where a small birthmark declared her the other half of Gideon's kind. She exhaled a soft laugh and shook her head. "Mama used to say it was a faerie's kiss."

Gideon stepped toward her where she sat on the old wooden chair. He gave a mild shrug. "Something made you and those others born with that mark different from other women. Who's to say it wasn't faeries?" His mouth curved in a tender, intimate smile. "It makes you very special, Savannah. Extraordinary. But you would be both those things and more, even without your mark."

Their eyes met and held for a long moment. Savannah watched, mesmerized, as the fiery sparks in his bright blue irises glittered like stars. His pupils had thinned to slender, vertical slits—inhuman, like a cat's eye. Maybe she should have been alarmed or repulsed; instead she was transfixed, astonished to see the change coming over him in so many intriguing, fantastical ways.

She reached out to him, invited him closer. He stepped between her knees and sank down on his haunches. His big body radiated a palpable heat. Where her knees and thighs touched him, she could feel the hard hammer of his pulse. Her own heartbeat seemed to answer it, falling into his rhythm as though they were one and the same being.

Savannah couldn't resist touching him.

His bare chest, shoulders, and powerful, muscled arms were alive with a tangle of intricate arcs and swirls that covered him, just a shade darker than his golden skin.

Dermaglyphs, he'd explained, along with the rest of what he'd told her.

She traced one of the patterns over his firm pectoral with her fingertip and marveled at how its color deepened at her touch. She followed the graceful swell and dip of the *glyph*, watching it come to life and flood from tawny gold to dark jewel tones.

"They're beautiful," she said, and heard his low rumble of approval deep in his chest as she teased more color into other places on his velvety skin. He had fascinated her from the moment she first met him under the Abbey murals at the library. But she was curious about him in a new way now. She wanted to know him better, wanted to know everything about her lover who was something much more than a man. "I could play with your *dermaglyphs* all day," she admitted, unable to hide her wonder and delight. "I love how the colors change to wine and indigo when I touch them."

"Desire," he rasped thickly. "That's what those colors mean."

She glanced up and saw a growing hunger in his handsome face, heard it in his low, rough-edged voice. "Your eyes," she said, noticing how the sparks had multiplied, now more of an amber glow, slowly swamping the blue of his irises. "When we made love earlier, I felt the heat of your gaze. I saw there was a fire coming to life in your eyes. This kind of fire. You hid it from me."

"I didn't want to frighten you." A flat, unabashed admission.

"I'm not afraid now, Gideon. I want to know." She reached out to him, cupped his rigid jaw in her palm. "I want to understand."

He stared at her for a long moment, then growled her name and covered her mouth in a long, slow kiss.

Savannah melted into him, swept up in the heat and pleasure of his lips on hers. She hungered for a deeper taste, testing the seam of his mouth with her tongue. He didn't give way to her at first, groaning as if to refuse her.

She wouldn't let him hide from her. Not now. Not again, not ever when they were together.

She scooted to the edge of the chair and wrapped her hands around the back of his head, spearing her fingers into the silk of his short hair. She traced her tongue along his mouth, insistent, pressing her body to his.

He gave up with a low curse and she pushed inside, thrilling to the feel of his hungered mouth.

The sharp tips of his fangs scraped her tongue as she kissed him deeper. When she could hardly take it any longer, she drew back to look him full in the face.

There was little left to confuse him with a mortal man. His eyes were blazing, fangs enormous and razor-sharp. His *dermaglyphs* were livid with dark color, churning like living things on his skin.

He was magnificent.

And she felt no fear as she drank in his full transformation.

"Take me to bed, Gideon. Make love to me again, now, like this. I want to be with you just the way you are."

With an otherworldly snarl of agreement, he swept her roughly off the seat and into his strong arms.

Then he rose and carried her into the bedroom as she'd commanded.

~ ~ ~

Gideon had never seen anything lovelier than the look of pleasure on Savannah's face as she climbed toward orgasm, her dark eyes locked on his gaze while she rode him in an unrushed, but slowly increasing, tempo.

They'd left the bed sometime before morning had dawned outside the sealed-up townhouse. Now, they sat face to face in a tub of warm bathwater, Savannah straddling him, his cock buried deep inside her tight sheath, her breasts dancing in tantalizing motion in front of his thirsting eyes and hungry mouth. He couldn't resist pulling one of the pert brown nipples between his teeth, rolling his tongue over the tight little peak and gently grazing the tip of his fangs along the supple curve of her flesh.

She drew in a sharp, shivery breath when he closed his mouth down on her a bit harder, just enough to remind her what he was and to torment himself with the want he felt to take things further with her—to make her his in every way.

Making love to her openly, without fear or concealment of his true nature, had been amazing. Mind-blowingly good. They had exhausted each other last night, sleeping for a short while in each other's arms before waking more than once to kiss and caress and make love all over again.

Gideon knew he should have broken away at some point to report in to the compound, but he hadn't been able to find the will to leave the bed he'd shared with Savannah. The way things were going this morning, he might never make it back. Savannah rocked on him, their eyes locked, her face aglow with the amber light of his pleasured gaze.

He stroked her face and throat as she moved on him in a deeper, faster rhythm. The bathwater lapped around them noisily, the sound of their lovemaking wet and erotic. She started to come then, soft moans slipping through her parted lips.

Gideon gripped her ass in a firmer hold and moved his pelvis in time with her undulations. His cock felt like hot steel inside the tight clutch of her body, pressure building to a fever pitch at the base of his spine. His fangs filled his mouth. His gums throbbed with the urge to taste the graceful column of Savannah's neck as she threw her head back and cried out with her climax.

Gideon followed her over the edge a moment later, his orgasm racking him in a full-body heave and a coarse shout of release. He shuddered inside her, wave after wave of scalding heat shooting out of him. He swore her name, prayer or curse, he didn't know.

She smiled as he filled her, her dark eyes drinking him in, even though he knew he must look savage and unearthly. She didn't shrink away. Not his Savannah, not now.

She slumped against him, limp and satiated. Gideon held her close, smoothing his hands along her back. Her breath was warm against the side of his neck, her lips soft and moist on the pulse point where she rested, making his carotid jump and pound in response.

"I can't get enough of you," she murmured. "Are you working some kind of Breed mojo on me that makes me want you so bad?"

He chuckled. "If only I had that kind of power. I'd never let you out of my bed. Or my bathtub."

"Or off the chair in the other room," she added, a reminder of yet another location they'd made use of in the past few blissful hours.

Gideon's arousal woke anew at the thought, and he wondered how intense their lovemaking would be if they were mated, sharing a blood bond. One little bite and she would be his forever. Dangerous thinking. Something he wasn't prepared to consider, no matter how much his body seemed to feel otherwise.

"I can't get enough of you, either," he told her, pressing a kiss to her temple. "It's been a long time since I've been with someone. I've had to remember all over again how it's done. Although I can't think of anything better than studying your body and learning all the ways to please you."

He felt her smile against him. "Well, you're doing everything right."

"I'm a fast study."

Savannah laughed and nestled in closer, mostly on top of him in the cramped, Victorian-era tub. Her long leg was draped over him, her arms wrapped around his chest. Gideon stroked her arm. "For a long time, I've been putting all of my energy and focus into the Order's missions. I'm definitely slacking there now. I'll likely have hell to pay—and rightly so—when I report back about where I've been."

Savannah lifted her head, studying his face. "How long?"

"How long since I've wanted anyone the way I want you?"

She nodded.

"Never," he said. "You're a first in that regard. I've had my share of liaisons. Thoughtless dalliances that meant nothing to me."

"How long since you've made love?" she pressed.

"The last time?" He shrugged. "Eighteen or nineteen years, if I had to guess." The span of her whole lifetime, which seemed somehow fitting to him now. "It wasn't memorable, Savannah. None of them were, compared to this. Compared to you."

She grew quiet, tracing a *glyph* on his chest. "I've only been with one guy before—Danny Meeks, a boy from my hometown. High school jock, varsity quarterback, homecoming king...the boy every girl in school dreamed of being with."

Gideon grunted, feeling a surge of bald possessiveness. He wanted to make a smartass comment about steakhead athletes with IQs smaller than his boot size, but he could sense Savannah holding back as she spoke.

"What did he do to you?" he asked, his possessiveness darkening toward fury with his suspicion that the stupid boy-man had wounded her somehow.

"I thought he really liked me. He had his pick of anyone he wanted in school, and he'd just broken up with the prettiest, most popular girl in my class. But there he was, pursuing me." She sighed softly, still moving her finger along the curve of Gideon's *dermaglyphs*, whose color was rising not in desire again, but anger for her pain. "We went on a few dates, and after several weeks, he started pressuring me to take things further with him. I was a virgin. I wanted to wait until I met the right one, you know?"

Gideon caressed her arm, letting her talk, while inside he knew where this was heading and he didn't like it.

"Finally, I gave in," she said. "We had sex, and it was awful. It hurt. He was clumsy and rough."

Gideon growled. He didn't want to imagine her with another man, let alone one who would be so careless with her.

"We dated for a couple of months afterward," she went on. "Danny never treated me any better. He just took what he wanted from me. After a while, I started hearing rumors that he had been calling his old girlfriend again. That he was only with me to make her jealous. They got back together, and I didn't even know about it until I saw them making out at one of his games. He never cared about me at all. He pretended to be one thing with me, but the whole time we were together, he was only using me to get something he really wanted."

"Bastard," Gideon snarled. He was pulsing with fury, wanting nothing better than to teach the little asshole a lesson. Throttle the human son of a bitch for hurting her. "Savannah, I'm sorry."

"It's okay." She shook her head where it rested against his chest. "I learned from it. It made me more careful. More protective of myself, of my heart. And then you came along..."

She looked up into his eyes. "I've never imagined I could feel all the things I feel with you, Gideon. I never understood how lost I've felt—all my life— until I found you. I think it must've been fate that brought us together at the library a few nights ago."

A pang of guilt stabbed him at the mention of how they'd first met. Only he knew it hadn't been fate at all that sent him to her that night. He'd first sought her out as a warrior on a private mission to gather intel on the sword and whoever had it now.

That mission had soon changed, once he came to know Savannah. Once he came to care about her so swiftly, so deeply. He should have come clean about their initial meeting before now. He should have done it right then—would have—but before he could summon the first word, she covered his mouth in a tender kiss.

It was all he could do not to end her sweet kiss and blurt out the other damning words that were on the tip of his tongue: *Be with me. Bond with me. Let me be your mate.*

But it wasn't fair to ask so much of her, not when she was just entering his world and he still had unfinished business to attend.

He still had hidden enemies to eliminate. And he wouldn't assume for one moment that killing the Rogue who'd accosted her at South Station removed the whole of the threat that was stalking Savannah.

Recalling that encounter made him go tense and sober. She must have felt the change in him, for Savannah drew back from him now. "What is it? What's wrong?"

"Last night, at the bus terminal," he said. "Did you notice anyone following you? Watching you, before or after you arrived? I don't mean the Rogue that cornered you, but someone else. Someone who might have been aware that it was happening."

"No. Why?" Apprehension flickered in her searching gaze. "Do you think the Rogue was with others? Do you think I was targeted somehow?"

"I think it's a very real possibility, Savannah. I'm not willing to assume otherwise." Gideon didn't want to alarm her unnecessarily, but she also had to understand how dangerous the situation could be for her outside. "I think the Rogue was sent to find you for someone else."

More than likely, sent to silence her, a thought that made his blood go icy in his veins.

Savannah stared at him. "Because of what happened to Rachel and Professor Keaton? You mean, you think the one who attacked them is now after me? Why?"

"The sword, Savannah. What else did you see when you touched it?"

She shook her head. "I told you. I saw the Rogues who killed those two little boys. And I saw you, striking someone with the blade. You killed someone with it."

Gideon gave a grim nod. "In a duel, many years ago, yes. I killed the Breed male who made the sword. His name was Hugh Faulkner, a Gen One Breed and the best sword maker in London at the time. He was also a prick and a bastard, a deviant who took his pleasure in bloodshed. Particularly when it came to human women."

"What happened?"

"One night in London, Faulkner showed up at a Cheapside tavern with a human female under his arm. She was in bad shape, pale and unresponsive, nearly bled out." Gideon couldn't curb the disgust in his tone. There were laws among his race meant to protect humans from the worst abuses of Breed power, but there were also individuals among their kind like Faulkner, those who regarded themselves above any law.

"Few of the Breed males in the establishment would consider rising up against a Gen One, especially one as nasty as Faulkner. But I couldn't abide what he had done to the woman. Words were exchanged. The next thing I knew, Faulkner and I were outside in the darkness, engaged in a contest to the death over the fate of the woman." Gideon recalled it as if the confrontation had just happened yesterday, not some three-hundred years in the past. "I had earned some renown for my skill with a sword, more so than Faulkner, as it turned out. He lost his blade almost immediately and stumbled. It was a fatal misstep. I could've taken his head then and there, but in an act of mercy—stupidity, in hindsight—I stayed my hand."

"He cheated?" Savannah guessed.

Gideon gave a vague nod. "The minute I turned to walk away and retrieve his fallen blade, Faulkner began to rise up to come at me. I realized my mistake at once. I recovered quickly—and before Faulkner could get to his feet, I rounded back on him and cleaved him in half with his own damned sword."

Savannah sucked in a soft breath. "That's what I saw. You, killing him with the sword I touched."

"I won the contest and sent the human woman away to be looked after until she was well again," Gideon replied. "As for Faulkner's sword, I wish I'd left it where it lay that night, next to his corpse."

Understanding dawned in Savannah's tender eyes. "The twin boys I saw playing with the sword before they were attacked in the stable by Rogues..."

"My brothers," he confirmed. "Simon and Roderick."

"Gideon," she whispered solemnly. "I'm sorry for your loss."

"A long time ago," he said.

"But you still feel it. Don't you?"

He released a heavy sigh. "I was to blame for not protecting them. Our parents were dead. The boys were my responsibility. Several weeks after the confrontation with Faulkner, I was out carousing in the city. Simon and Roddy were young, not even ten years old, but old enough to hunt on their own as Breed youths. I took it for granted that they'd be safe enough on their own for a few hours that night."

Savannah reached over and pulled his fisted hand up to her lips, kissed the tightly clenched knuckles with sweet compassion. He relaxed his fingers to twine them with hers. "My brothers were the reason I came to Boston. I joined the Order t hunt Rogues, after killing the three who murdered the boys, as well as dozens more for good measure."

"Hundreds more," Savannah reminded him.

He grunted. "I thought killing Rogues would make the guilt about my brothers lessen, but it hasn't."

"How long have you been trying to make it better, Gideon?"

He exhaled a low oath. "Simon and Roddy were killed three centuries ago."

She lifted her head up and stared at him. Gaped at him. "Exactly how old are you?"

"Three-hundred and seventy-two," he drawled. "Give or take a few months."

"Oh, my God." She dropped her head back down on his chest and laughed. Then laughed again. "I thought Rachel was nuts for lusting after Professor Keaton, and he was only in his forties. I'm falling in love with a total relic."

Gideon stilled. "Falling in love?"

"Yes," she replied quietly, but without hesitation. She glanced up at him. One slender black brow arched wryly. "Don't tell me that's all it takes to scare a three-hundred and seventy-two-year-old vampire."

"No," he said, but he did feel a sudden wariness.

Not because of her sweet confession; he would come back to that tempting pronouncement another time.

Right now, his warrior instincts were buzzing with cold alarm. He sat up in the tub, frowning.

"Keaton," he said flatly. "When is he due out of the hospital?"

"He is out," Savannah replied. "I saw him yesterday on campus. He looked awful, but he said he'd made a full recovery and the hospital released him earlier than expected. He was acting kind of odd—"

Gideon tensed. "Odd in what way?"

"I don't know. Weird. Creepy. And he lied to me when I asked him about the attack."

"Tell me."

She shrugged. "He told me he saw who killed Rachel and attacked him that night. Keaton said it was a vagrant, but the glimpse I got from Rachel's bracelet showed me a man in a very expensive suit. A man with amber eyes and fangs."

"Holy shit." Why he didn't see it before, Gideon had no idea. The attacker killed Savannah's roommate, but left the professor alive. That was no accident. "What else did Keaton say to you?"

"Nothing much. Like I said, he was just acting strangely, not like himself. I didn't feel safe around him."

"Did Keaton know you were going to the bus station last night?"

She paused, thinking. "I told him I was going home to Louisiana. I might have mentioned I was taking the bus—"

Gideon snarled and got out of the tub. Water sluiced off his naked limbs and torso. "I need to see Keaton for myself. It's the only way I can be certain." He thought about the hour of the day—probably just past noon—and cursed roundly.

Savannah climbed out too, and stood beside him. She put her hand on his shoulder. "Gideon, what do you need to be certain of?"

"Keaton's injuries the night of the attack," he said. "I need to know if he was bitten."

"I don't know. I didn't see that much when I touched Rachel's bracelet." She stared at him in confusion. "Why? What will it tell you if Keaton was bitten?"

"If I see him, I'll know right away if he's still human or if he's been bitten and bled by his attacker. I need to know if he's been made a Minion to the vampire who took that sword from the university."

"A Minion." Savannah went quiet now. "If Keaton was bitten, that will tell you what you need to know?"

"Yes." He raked a hand over his scalp. "The problem with that is, I'm trapped indoors until sundown."

"Gideon," she said. "What if I see Keaton now?"

"What do you mean?" He bristled at the thought of her getting anywhere near the man. "You're not going anywhere without me. I won't risk that."

She shook her head. "I mean, maybe I can tell you if Keaton was bitten during the attack." At his answering scowl, she said, "I still have Rachel's bracelet."

"Where?"

"Here, with me. It's in my purse in the other room."

"I need you to go get it, Savannah. Now."

CHAPTER 13

Savannah woke up from an unusually heavy doze, in bed alone.

How long had she been asleep? Her head felt thick, like she was coming out of a light anesthesia.

Where was Gideon?

She called out to him, but the empty house was silent. Pushing herself up from the mattress, she made a bleary-eyed scan of the dark bedroom. "Gideon?"

No response.

"Gideon, where are you?"

She sat up and tossed the sheet away from her. Turned on the bedside lamp. On the pillow next to her lay a piece of paper. A note scribbled on the back of the unused bus ticket that had been in her purse. The handwriting was crisp, precise, forward-tilting and bold—just like him.

Sorry had to do it like this. You're safe here. Back soon.

Savannah looked around the bedroom. Gideon's clothes were gone. His boots and weapons. Every last trace of him, gone.

She knew where he went.

Through the fog of whatever he'd done to her, she recalled his explosive reaction when she'd used Rachel's bracelet for another glimpse of the vampire attack that night in Professor Keaton's office.

Keaton had been bitten, just as Gideon suspected.

No longer the man he was, but a slave to the command of his vampire Master.

An individual Gideon seemed hellbent to find.

He had nearly climbed the walls with restless energy as the afternoon dragged on outside the house. He couldn't wait to get out of there. He'd paced anxiously, waiting for the chance to head out and confront Keaton, then hunt for the Minion's Master.

Savannah had wanted to go with him, but his refusal had been harsh and unswerving. He'd been adamant that she stay right where she was, leave him to deal with the situation as he saw fit—alone. Or with his brethren of the Order, if necessary.

It wasn't until she had insisted she wouldn't stay behind, digging her heels in with determination equal to his own that he finally gentled.

He'd kissed her tenderly. Brought her into the shelter of his arms, and carefully touched his palm to her forehead. Then...

Then, nothing.

That's all she could remember of the past couple of hours at least.

Sorry had to do it like this, he'd written in his note.

Damn him!

Savannah vaulted off the bed. She threw on her clothes, ran to the front door. She yanked on the latch. It wouldn't budge.

He'd locked her inside?

Pissed now, she went to the windows and tried to open them. Sealed permanently shut, each of them shuttered from outside. The whole house was locked down, she realized, making a frantic perimeter check of the entire place.

She finally came to a rest in the small, empty kitchen, breathless with outrage.

There was no way to get out.

She was imprisoned here, and Gideon was somewhere out there, looking to face off with a powerful enemy on his own.

She knew she couldn't help him—not in the kind of battles he was used to fighting. But to leave her behind like this to wait and worry? To strong-arm her into complying with his will by flexing his Breed power over her? If she wasn't so worried about him, she'd want to kill him herself the next time she saw him.

She choked back a panicky breath. *God, please, let me see him again.*

She sagged down to the rough plank floor on her knees...and noticed something in the far corner of the kitchen that she hadn't seen in her search for a means out of the house.

There was a door in the floor.

Hardly visible, fashioned out of the planks and perfectly level with the rest of the flooring.

With a mix of curiosity and foreboding, Savannah crept toward it and felt around for its seams. She pried her fingers between a couple of the planks and found the hidden, square panel was unhinged and unsecured. She lifted it, slid it aside, and sat back as a draft of cool, damp air breathed out of the dark opening.

Savannah peered down into the space, trying to see if it the gloom led out of the house somewhere, or merely down to an old cellar. A prickle at her nape told her it was neither, but now that she had opened the door, she couldn't simply close it again without having the answer.

A crude ladder was built into the earthen wall below. She slipped down into the hole and carefully climbed about twenty feet to the bottom.

It was a deep pit, lightless, except for the scant illumination spilling in from the kitchen above.

Had she thought the house felt like a tomb last night, when she and Gideon first arrived? This hand-hewn chamber in the cold, dark earth brought the feeling back tenfold.

Who made this?

What was it for?

Savannah peered around the forlorn space. Nothing but dank walls and floor, a place of sorrow and isolation. A place of forgetting.

No, she thought, seeing the purpose of the hidden room only now—a niche carved into the far wall, created to hold the crude wooden box that had been carefully placed within the nook.

This hole in the earth was a place of remembrance.

Of penance.

She drifted closer to the alcove and the aged box it contained. Even without touching it, she could feel the anguish that surrounded the reliquary.

Where had the box come from? Why was it here? Who had set it so deliberately in this place?

She had to know.

Savannah ran her bare hand lightly over the top of the ancient box.

Grief swamped her, seeping straight to her marrow.

A young woman's remains were inside from long, long ago. Ash and bone, anointed in tears. A man's tears.

No, not a man.

A Breed male, unfamiliar to her, mourning his dead mate. Blaming himself for her demise.

Savannah saw him in a flash of her extrasensory gift: A massive warrior with shaggy, tawny hair and piercing gem-green eyes. Eyes that burned hot with rage and sorrow and self-loathing.

His pain was too much, too raw.

Too wrenching for her to take any longer.

She drew her hand away in a hurry and backed off, putting as much distance as she could between herself and the terrible past contained in the box.

Shaken, wanting no more knowledge of this house's hidden rooms or secrets, she ran back upstairs to wait for Gideon's return.

~ ~ ~

After pulling a B&E on the Faculty Administration building at the university as soon as night had fallen, Gideon headed into the working-class neighborhood of Southie, his sights set on the home of one Professor William Charles Keaton.

The run-down, turn-of-the-century New Englander didn't exactly scream swinging bachelor pad, but there was a flashy white Firebird parked on the side driveway that was advertisement enough for a coed skirt-chaser like Keaton.

Or rather, a skirt-chaser like he had been.

After hearing Savannah confirm that afternoon what Gideon had suspected—that Keaton had, in fact, been bitten by the Breed male who attacked him—Gideon was pretty sure the only thing that interested Keaton now was obeying his Master's orders.

Gideon needed to know who Keaton served.

He needed to know who wanted Hugh Faulkner's sword bad enough to kill for it, and why.

He wasn't holding out much hope that Keaton would give up those answers easily, if at all. Interrogating Minions wasn't often the most productive effort. A mind slave's allegiance belonged totally to its Master.

Still, Gideon had to try.

For Savannah's safety, if nothing else.

He'd hated like hell to have to resort to trancing her just before sundown, but he didn't see where he'd had much choice. He never would have gotten out of that house without her. Locking her inside probably wasn't going to win him any hero awards, either.

Shit.

He'd have to add another apology to the rest he owed her—starting with the one he planned to open with as soon as he saw her again.

The one about how he'd let her go on thinking all this time that the way they first met had been simple serendipity. Fate, as she'd christened it, just before her sweet confession that she was falling in love with him.

She needed to know that despite his reasons for seeking her out in the beginning, what he felt for her now—immediately after meeting her, if he were being honest with himself—was real.

She needed to know that she mattered to him, even more than his personal quest for answers about the damned sword and the Breed male who'd been willing to kill for it.

She needed to know that he loved her.

He didn't know a better way to prove that than removing the threat of anyone who sought to do her harm.

Starting with the Minion inside this house.

Gideon entered stealthily, the feeble lock on the old front door no contest at all for the mental command he gave that opened it. A television blared unattended in the living room just off the entryway. A day-old dinner sat dried out in its foil container on the TV tray next to a cushioned brown recliner. Spread open on the seat was a state map of Louisiana.

Son of a bitch.

Gideon had to clamp down hard on the fury that began to boil in his gut as he noted the penciled line tracing down to the south central region of the state.

He swept his gaze all around him, searching for the bodily energy of the house's occupant with his ESP talent. He found Keaton's faint orange glow beneath the floorboards at his feet. The Minion was in the cellar.

Gideon stalked toward the hallway stairwell leading to the basement below.

A dim light was on down there.

Sounds of vague rummaging filtered up the steps...then, abrupt silence.

The Minion had just clued in to the presence of a Breed male other than his Master.

Gideon had one of his guns in hand as he descended the stairs into an open area of the basement. Keaton was gone, fled somewhere to hide, no doubt. Not that he could get far.

Gideon walked down, his gaze straying to a rough-hewn workbench and wallboard hung with home improvement tools and small containers of supplies. A dark duffel bag sat open on the bench. Inside it were coils of rope, a hunting knife, a roll of silver duct tape.

Gideon's blood seethed at the sight of an obvious abduction kit.

Keaton's Master had apparently changed his mind about siccing Rogues on Savannah and now wanted her taken alive. The thought didn't sit any better with Gideon.

He swung his head around the cluttered basement, looking for the Minion.

Found him lurking in a back room of the space.

Gideon strode forward, toward a connected room separated by a beaded curtain. He swept it aside and entered a room decorated in what could only be described as Assorted Early Warfare. The walls sported an extensive collection of muskets and maces, rapiers and powder horns. Evidently, Keaton preferred his history with a dash of bloodshed.

Gideon stalked toward the glow of Keaton's form, concealed behind a closet door at the far end of the room. Gideon wanted to blast a hole in the bastard through the wood panel, but he needed the

Minion breathing so he could wring the name of his Master from him.

"Planning a road trip, Keaton?" he asked.

No reply. The Minion made small, urgent movements inside the closet, movements Gideon saw as slight shifts of the human's energy mass. He couldn't kill Keaton outright, but taking off a limb at a time might prove his point.

"We need to have a talk, Keaton. You need to tell me who you serve."

The Minion snickered now. Gideon blew out a curse and shook his head. "You can come out now, or you can come out in pieces."

Again, no response. So Gideon fired a shot into the door.

The Minion grunted upon the impact, but hardly reacted to the pain. Then he started chuckling. Tittering maniacally.

Gideon realized his mistake only a fraction of a second too late.

Keaton opened the closet door. He was smiling, holding two World War II-era grenades in his hands. The pins were already gone.

Holy Christ.

Gideon turned and sped in the other direction.

Made it halfway up the stairs just as the grenades detonated.

The blast threw him into the wall, smoke and debris flying all around him. He hit hard, felt the burn of random shrapnel peppering his back. But he was alive. He was still in one piece. Relief washed over him...until his nostrils filled with the alarming scent of his own blood.

A lot of it.

He shifted from where he had fallen on the stairs and looked down to assess the damage. Hundreds of lacerations and singed skin where the hot shrapnel had hit him. Nothing his Breed genetics couldn't heal on their own in a few hours' time.

But it was the other wound that gave him pause.

The catastrophic rip in his left thigh, which had nearly severed the limb and was currently gushing like a geyser with each heavy pound of his heartbeat.

Blood seeped out of him fast and hard.

His body could mend itself from injury. It had, more times than he'd ever bothered to remember.

But this was bad.

This was deadly bad, even for one of his kind.

CHAPTER 14

A heavy thump hit the front door, drawing Savannah up from the chair with a start. Gideon?

It seemed like she'd been waiting forever, concern for him and distress over being left alone in the sorrowful old house making time drag endlessly.

Another loud thump sounded from outside the door.

She crossed the room, feeling a surge of relief. "Gideon, is that you?"

She wanted it to be him.

Prayed it was...until she heard the metallic snick of the lock, then the door opened and a large, blood-and-sweat-soaked body slumped in onto the floor.

"Oh, my God. Gideon!"

Savannah raced to him. She dropped down beside him, horrified at his condition. His hair and face, his hands—every exposed inch of him was covered in black ash, sweat and blood. So much blood.

He tried to speak, but all that passed his lips was a rasp of sound. "Keaton," he wheezed. "Minion...he's dead...can't hurt you now."

She blew out a curse that sounded more like a sob. "I don't care about him, damn it. All I care about is you."

He tried to sit up, only to slump back down onto the floor in a heap. Blood was pooling under him, pulsing out from scores of shrapnel wounds and a very severe injury in his thigh.

She glanced down at his leather weapons belt, cinched as a makeshift tourniquet around the upper portion of his leg. She could see muscle in the open gash on his thigh. Holy shit. She could see bone in there too.

"Gideon," she cried. "You need help. You need a hospital—"

"No." He snarled the word, his voice sounding unearthly, lethal.

His eyes were on fire, swamped completely in bright, glowing amber light. His pupils had thinned so much they almost weren't there. His fangs filled his mouth, stretched sharp as daggers between his parted lips as he struggled to drag air into his lungs.

"Get away," he gasped when she reached out to smooth away the soaked hank of hair plastered to his brow. His skin was pale white and waxy. His face contorted in pure agony. "Stay away."

"You have to let me help you." She leaned over him to try to lift him up.

Gideon's eyes rolled hungrily to her throat. "Stay back!"

The hissed command made her flinch, recoil. She stared at him, unsure what to do for him and half-afraid he was already too far gone.

"Gideon, please. I don't know what to do."

"Order," he said thickly. He recited a string of numbers. "Go now...call them."

She tried desperately to remember the sequence, repeated them back to him to be sure. He gave a vague nod, his eyelids drooping, skin growing ever more dangerously pale. "Hurry, Savannah."

"Okay," she said. "Okay, Gideon. I'll call them. Stay with me. I'm gonna get you help."

She flew into the bedroom to retrieve her wallet from her purse and a pen to frantically scribble the digits onto the palm of her hand. Then she raced out of the house and down the street, praying the battered pay phone on the corner wasn't out of service.

Fumbling change into the slot, she then dialed the number Gideon had given her. It rang once, then silence as someone picked up on the other end.

"Um, hello? Hello!"

"Yeah." A deep voice. Dark, arresting. Menacing.

"Gideon told me to call," she blurted in one panicked rush of breath. "Something's happened to him and I—"

Click.

"Hello?"

The dial tone buzzed in her ear.

~ ~ ~

It wasn't even ten minutes later that Savannah found herself standing beside an unresponsive Gideon, staring up into the hard face and unreadable eyes of a massive Breed male dressed in black leather and pulsing with lethal power.

He hadn't knocked, simply strode right in without a word of greeting or explanation. And he'd arrived on foot apparently, from where, Savannah could only guess.

Since she'd met Gideon and learned about his kind, she was coming to simply accept some things as simply part of the new reality.

Still, she could hardly curb the impulse to scrabble out of the disturbing male's way when he came farther inside the house.

The place was his, there could be no doubt about that.

He was the one who put the box of ashes in the hidden room below the kitchen.

It was his wrenching sorrow Savannah had glimpsed when she touched the reliquary.

He stared at her now without any emotion whatsoever. His green eyes didn't so much look at her as through her.

He knew. He knew she'd been down in his private cell filled with death.

Savannah could see the awareness of her breach all over his grim face, although he said nothing to her. Did nothing, except grimly go to Gideon's side. He bent his big body and went down in a crouch on his haunches beside Gideon. A low curse hissed out of big male.

"He won't wake up," Savannah murmured. "After I came back from making the call, I found him like this, unconscious."

"He's lost too much blood." The voice was the same deep, threatening growl that she'd heard on the other end of the line. "He needs proper care."

"Can you save him?"

The tawny head swiveled to face her, bleak green eyes raking her. "He needs blood."

Savannah glanced down at Gideon, recalling his sharp reprimand that she not come near him. He'd been furious, desperately so, even though it had been obvious that he wanted to drink from her—needed to. "He didn't want me. He told me to stay away from him."

That unsettling stare stayed locked on her for a long moment before the vampire returned his attention to his fallen comrade. He inspected Gideon's leg wound, snarling as he assessed the damage. "So, you're the girl."

"Excuse me?"

"The Breedmate my man here hasn't been able to stay away from since he saw you on the TV news earlier this week, talking about the sword used to kill his brothers."

Savannah felt a twinge of confusion. An odd niggle of dread. "Gideon saw me on the news? He knew I'd seen the sword?" She shook her head. "No, that's not right. We met at the library where I work. He didn't know anything about me before then."

The other warrior glanced over at her once more, a flat look that made her discomfort deepen even more.

"Gideon was looking at some of the library's artwork. It was just before closing, and..."

Her words drifted off as an unwanted realization began to settle on her.

Right. He just happened to be at the library, not looking for books, but browsing artwork outside her office. Flirting with her. Quoting Plutarch and practically charming her pants off under the Abbey Room murals.

Pretending he knew nothing about the fact that her roommate had been murdered the night before by a goddamn vampire—one of his own kind.

Savannah felt oddly exposed. Like a fool who had arrived two minutes after a punch line.

"Are you saying he sought me out that night?"

The warrior swore, low under his breath, but he didn't answer her question. There was no need. She knew the truth now. Finally, she supposed.

Gideon had seen her interview on the news and pursued her to get information on someone he was determined to find. Someone he believed was his enemy, perhaps connected to the murders of his brothers.

He'd used her.

That's why he knew where she lived, why he was always in the right place at the right time with her.

He was tracking her the way he would any other prey...or pawn.

God, was everything between them just part of some plan? Some private vendetta he meant to pursue?

Savannah staggered backward a pace, feeling as if she'd just been slapped.

He was still using her today, encouraging her to touch Rachel's bracelet so he could learn more about Keaton and the vampire who'd attacked him.

Now Gideon was lying there at her feet, wounded and weak, unconscious and bleeding—maybe dying—because of his damned quest.

And she was standing over him like an idiot, feeling helpless and afraid...terrified that she had let herself fall in love with him, when all she'd apparently been to him was a means to an end.

It was easier to accept that he was Breed—something far other than human—than it was to realize she'd been played this whole time. The hurt she felt was like cold steel in the center of her being.

One other person had used her to get something he wanted more, but Danny Meeks had only taken her virginity. Gideon had taken her heart.

Savannah took a step back. Then another, watching as Gideon's comrade from the Order adjusted the tourniquet around his savaged thigh and prepared to carry him back to where he belonged.

She felt cool air at her back as she edged out the open door and into the night.

Then she pivoted and bolted, before the first hot tears began to flood her cheeks.

CHAPTER 15

*S*avannah.*"

Gideon jolted back to wakefulness on a shout, his sole concern, his every cell, honed in on a single thought...*her.*

He sat up and felt the sharp stab of pain answer from all over his body, the worst of it coming from the deep gash in his thigh. He was in a bed. Lying in the Order's infirmary. He breathed in, and didn't smell any of the ash or sweat or blood that had crusted every square inch of him following his ordeal at the Minion's house. Someone had gone to the trouble of cleaning him up after patching him back together.

"What time is it?" he murmured out loud. How long had he been unconscious? "Ah, shit. What day is it?"

"It's okay, Gideon. Relax." A gentle female hand settled on his bare shoulder. "You're okay. Tegan brought you back to the compound last night."

Last night.

"Danika," he rasped, peeling his eyes open to look up at Conlan's Breedmate, who stood beside him, a roll of white gauze bandages in her hand. "Where is she? Where's Savannah?"

The tall blonde gave a sympathetic shake of her head. "I'm sorry, I don't know."

Damn it. Gideon threw off the sheet and swung his legs around to the side of the bed, ignoring the hot, spearing complaint of his wounds. "I need to see her. I need to find her. Keaton's Master is still out there somewhere. She's not safe—"

"She's gone, man." Tegan stood at the threshold of the infirmary room. His face was grim, barely an acknowledgment as Danika quietly slipped out and left the two warriors alone. "My fault, Gideon. I didn't know—"

"What happened?" A spike of adrenaline and dread shot into his veins. "What did you do to her?"

"Told her the truth. Which is apparently more than you'd done."

"Ah, fuck." Gideon raked a hand through his hair. "Fuck me. What did you tell her, T?"

A vague shrug, although his green eyes stayed unreadable. "That she's been your personal obsession since you saw her on that newscast the day of the attack at the university."

Gideon groaned. "Shit."

"Yeah, she wasn't exactly happy to hear that."

"I have to go to her. She could be in danger, Tegan. I need to find her and make sure she's all right. I have to make sure she knows that I love her. That I need her."

"You're not in any condition to leave the compound."

"Fuck that." Gideon heaved onto his feet, grimacing at the agony of his wounded leg, but not about to let something as trivial as a recently severed femoral artery keep him from going after the woman he loved. "She's mine. She belongs with me. I'm going to tell her that, and then I'm going to bring her back."

Tegan grunted. "Kind of figured you might say that. And I'm way ahead of you, my man—for once, maybe. Got the Order's charter jet on standby, fueled up and waiting for you at the private hangar. You just need to tell the pilots where you want to go."

"Louisiana," he murmured. "She'll have gone home to Louisiana."

Tegan tossed him a stack of fresh clothing that had been set next to the bed. "What are you waiting for, then? Get the fuck outta here."

~ ~ ~

With the thick shadows of the Atchafalaya swamp looming up ahead, Gideon hopped off the back of the old pickup truck he'd hitched a ride on outside the Baton Rouge airport. His leg wound ached like a son of a bitch with every mile he ran, deeper into the dense vegetation and drooping, moss-laden cypress trees of the basin.

Savannah's sister, Amelie, lived on a remote road in this sparsely populated stretch of marshlands. Gideon knew precisely where to find her; after waking in the infirmary, he'd lingered at the Order's compound only long enough to run a quick hack on the IRS databases, which coughed up her address in no time at all.

He crept off an unpaved road to stalk up on the modest, gray-shingled house with its covered porch and soft-glowing light in the windows. There were no cars in the unpaved driveway out front. No sound coming from within the small abode as he stole toward it.

He climbed up the squat steps leading to the porch and front door, his thigh muscle protesting each flex and movement. His talent reached past the thin walls of the house, searching for telltale life energy. Someone sat in the living room, alone.

Gideon knocked on the front door—only to discover it wasn't closed all the way.

"Savannah?"

A muffled groan answered from inside.

"Savannah!" Gideon had his gun in his hand now, storming into the place, his body filled with alarm.

It wasn't Savannah. Her sister, no doubt. The early middle-aged black woman was bound and gagged on a kitchen chair in the center of the living room. Evidence of a scuffle were all around her, toppled furniture, broken knick-knacks.

But no sign of Savannah.

Amelie Dupree's eyes went wide as Gideon approached her with the pistol gripped in his fist. She screamed through the gag, started to flail in panic on the chair.

"Shh," Gideon soothed, working past his terror for what might have happened to Savannah. He tore Amelie's bonds loose and freed the cloth from around her face and mouth. "I'm not going to hurt you. Where's Savannah? I'm here to protect her."

"They took her!"

Gideon's blood ran cold. "Who took her?"

"I don't know." She shook her head, a sob cracking in her throat. "Couple of men came here, showed up about an hour ago. Tied me up and they took my baby sister away at gunpoint."

Gideon's growl of rage was animalistic, lethal. "Where did they take her? What did these men look like?"

Amelie sagged forward, her head in her hands. "I don't know, I don't know! Oh, God, somebody gotta help her. I gotta call the police!"

Gideon took the woman's shoulders in a firm grasp, compelling her to look at him. "Listen to me, Amelie. You have to stay put, call no one. You have to trust me. I'm not going to let anything happen to Savannah."

She stared at him, doubt swimming in her anguished eyes. "Are you the one? Are you the one who broke her heart back there in Boston, sent her back here last night like her whole world was falling apart?"

He didn't answer to that, even though the blame settled heavily on him. "I'm the one who loves her. More than life itself."

"Don't let them hurt her," she cried. "Don't let those men kill my sweet Savannah."

Gideon gave a solemn shake of his head. "I won't. I swear my life on that."

No sooner had he said it, a vehicle approached, pulling up alongside the house outside. The dull rumble of the engine went silent, followed by the crisp thump of two car doors closing a moment later.

Gideon lifted his head, every battle instinct coming alive inside him. He whirled around to head out the front door, his gun at the ready.

There she was.

Standing on her sister's front lawn in the darkness, caught in a headlock by a human man—a Minion, Gideon realized at once. The big thug held the nose of his pistol jammed up against Savannah's temple. She'd been crying, her face streaked with tears, lips ashen from terror.

All the blood rushed out of Gideon's head, started pounding hard in the center of his chest.

It was then he noticed the second man, a Breed male, standing at ease in the shadows of a cypress tree nearby. He was dressed in a tailored navy wool overcoat, his brown hair impeccably cut, and swept back elegantly from his face. Held in a loose grasp in front of him stood a gleaming length of polished steel. The long blade glittered in the moonlight.

Gideon didn't need to see the hilt to know there would be a bird of prey—a falcon—tooled into the handcrafted grip.

Hugh Faulkner's blade.

But this was not the Gen One sword smith Gideon killed back in London all those centuries ago. He'd never seen this vampire before, he was certain.

"Drop your weapons, warrior."

Gideon glanced from the Breed male to the Minion holding Savannah, calculating which of the two he should kill first to give her the best odds of getting away unharmed. Neither was a guarantee, and he was loath to risk making a mistake that carried such a high cost.

"Put them down now," the vampire drawled. "Or my man will blow her pretty head off."

Gideon relaxed his hold on the pistol, then stooped to set it down.

"All of them. Slowly."

He took off his weapons belt and put it on the ground at his feet. The bandaged gash on his thigh was bleeding again, seeping through his pant leg.

The other vampire sniffed the air dramatically, lips peeling back in an amused smirk. "Not so untouchable, after all."

Gideon watched the Breed male turn Faulkner's sword on its tip in the moist earth of Amelie Dupree's front yard. "Do I know you?"

The vampire chuckled. "No one did. Not back then."

Gideon tried to place him, tried to figure out if, or when, their paths might have crossed.

"You wouldn't have noticed me. He hardly did, either." There was an acid resentment in the tone, but something else too. An old, bitter hurt. "His unacknowledged bastard. The only kin he had."

Gideon narrowed his gaze on the other male. "Hugh Faulkner had a son?"

A thin, hate-filled smile stretched the polished facade of his face into an ugly sneer. "A teenage son who watched him die at your hand, slaughtered in the open with less regard than might be shown common swine. A son who vowed to avenge him, even thought he had no use for me in life." Hugh Faulkner's bastard smiled a true smile now. "A son who decided to take from my father's killer the only family he had left too."

Gideon bristled, fury spiking in his veins. "My brothers were innocent children. You arranged for those three Rogues to go in and murder them?"

"I thought it would be enough," he replied evenly. "I thought it would settle the score. And it did, for a long time. Even after I came to America to begin a new life under a new name. A name I built into something prestigious, something respectable: Cyril Smithson."

Gideon vaguely recalled the name from among those of the Darkhaven elite. A wealthy, socially important name. One that could be destroyed within the Breed's civilian circles, if word of its patriarch's ignoble, murderous past were to come to light.

"Knowing I took your last living kin might have been enough, even after I found myself in Boston and watched you carrying out your missions as one of the Order," Smithson went on. "But then my do-gooder Breedmate foolishly donated some of my private things to the university, including my father's sword. When I went to retrieve it, Keaton was in his office pounding into a young slut. She saw me and screamed." The Breed male clucked his tongue. "Well, I couldn't be blamed for what happened next. The girl saw my fangs, my eyes."

"So you killed her too," Gideon said.

Smithson shrugged. "She had to be dealt with. Her roommate, here too."

Gideon followed the vampire's glance toward Savannah. She was breathing hard, breast rising and falling rapidly in her fear. Her eyes locked on to Gideon's, pleading, praying.

Smithson spun the sword idly with his fingers. "This blade was never supposed to leave my possession after the Rogues brought it to me with your brothers' blood on it. You were never supposed to know the truth of what happened that night. Now that you do...well, I suppose it's all come back around to the beginning again, hasn't it?"

The vampire lifted the sword, testing its weight. "I'd never been much good with blades. Crude weapons, really. But effective."

"What do you want, Smithson? A contest to the death with me, here and now?"

"Yes." He met Gideon's seething gaze across the yard. "Yes, that's precisely what I want. But I won't underestimate you the way my father did."

He slanted a look at his Minion. Two shots rang out in rapid succession, a bullet for each of Gideon's shoulders.

Savannah screamed. She struggled in her captor's hold now, her eyes tearing up as she looked at Gideon and the barrel of the Minion's pistol came back to her temple.

He barely felt the pain of the new wounds. His focus was rooted wholly on her, and on the wild, desperate expression in her gaze. He gave a faint shake of his head, unspoken command that she not do anything to risk her own life.

"That ought to level the playing field," Smithson remarked as the gunshots continued to echo through the bayou. "On second thought, another for good measure," he told his Minion. "The gut this time."

The Minion's hand started to move away from Savannah's head. Gideon saw it in agonizing slow motion—the twitch of muscle as the human's wrist began to pivot from its primary target to the new one at his Master's command.

Savannah, no!

Gideon didn't even have time to bring the words to his tongue. She seized the opportunity to shift her weight as the Minion's attention flicked away from her. Savannah knocked the man's arm up, just as he pulled the trigger. The shot went wild, up into the trees, and Savannah broke loose of the Minion's hold.

"Kill her," Smithson ordered.

And in one awful, shattering instant, another bullet blasted out of the Minion's gun. It hit her in the back. Dropped her like dead weight to the ground.

Amelie shrieked and flew off the porch behind him to race to her sister's side.

Gideon roared. Horror and rage bled through him, cold and black and acrid. "No!" he howled, racked with an anguish unlike any he'd ever known. "No!"

He leapt on Smithson, took him down in a hard crash to the ground.

He pounded and beat him, the pair of vampires rolling around in a savage hand-to-hand struggle in the wet grass. Gideon was vaguely aware of the Minion racing toward them, the barrel of his pistol aimed down at the scuffle, but hesitant to shoot and inadvertently snuff his own maker.

Gideon ignored the threat and kept up his punishment of Smithson. They tore at each other, gnashing with fangs and teeth as they wrestled on the ground. Gideon's fury was a hungry beast, waiting for the chance to deal the final blow.

When Smithson turned his head to reach for his lost blade, Gideon pounced with lethal purpose. He grabbed hold of the other male's throat with his teeth and fangs, sinking them deep.

He bit down hard into Smithson's neck, ripping out flesh and larynx in one savage shake of his head.

Smithson jerked and flailed in agony, blood spurting everywhere.

His Minion stood in stunned silence, a brief hesitation that was all the time Gideon needed to finish them both in one strike.

He picked up Faulkner's sword and drove it into Smithson's chest.

The vampire convulsed around the blade, eyes going wide and bulging in their sockets.

Gideon heard another round of gunfire somewhere close to him. Felt a sudden, hard knock in the side of his skull, before his vision began to fill with red. Blood. His blood, pouring into his eyes from the hole now bored into his skull from the Minion's final shot.

Smithson's chest rattled with a wet, gurgling breath as death took him under. His Minion dropped lifeless to the ground at the same time, the mind slave's life tied inexorably to his Master's.

"Savannah." Gideon dragged himself over to where Amelie hovered at her side. Savannah wasn't moving. Her back was covered in blood. The gunshot wound a dark hole burned through her pale gray sweater, up near her ribs.

"She's dying!" Amelie wailed, not looking at him, but focused completely on her sister. She petted Savannah with trembling hands, her face stricken with sorrow. "You promised to save her. You swore on your life."

"Move aside," he rasped thickly, his voice unearthly, ragged from injury and anguish and the crowding presence of his fangs, which filled his mouth. "Let me help her."

It was only then that Amelie turned to look at him. She sucked in a sharp breath and recoiled. She scrabbled backward with Savannah held close to her as if she thought she could protect her from the monster, bleeding and hideously transformed from the man he'd been just a few minutes ago. "Oh, my God. What kind of devil's spawn are you?"

"Please," Gideon hissed. His vision was fading, his pulse hammering heavily in his temples, bringing excruciating pain to his skull. He had to act quickly. There wasn't much time to do what was needed before one or the other of them died. He reached for Savannah's hand, gently took her limp form out of Amelie's grasp. "Please, it's the only way. Trust me in this. Let me save her."

He didn't wait. Couldn't let another second tick by without feeding the power of his blood to Savannah's wounds.

He bit into his wrist and held the opened vein over her parted lips.

"Drink," he whispered thickly. "Please, baby...drink for me."

Deep red droplets splashed down into her slack mouth. The stream picked up speed, pulsing out of him with every labored beat of his heart. "Come on, Savannah. Do it. Please take this gift from me. It's all I have to give you now."

Her tongue began to flick softly. Her slender throat began to work, taking the first swallow from his vein. She drank again, then another. Her eyelids started to lift slightly, just a hint of response, but enough to wring a sigh of naked relief out of Gideon's chest.

She would survive.

He felt it with a certainty that humbled him. His blood would save her.

She was alive. Smithson was dead, unable to harm her.

Gideon had kept his promise to her, after all.

His vision faded from dull gray to black, a numbness creeping over his scalp. He had to struggle to remain upright, invisible tethers dragging him down.

He fought the heavy pull of his injury and cradled Savannah's head in his arm, centering himself with the steady rhythm of her mouth working softly at his wrist, drinking from him, healing because of him.

For now, that was enough.

CHAPTER 16

Savannah was resting in a chair in the back bedroom of Amelie's house when Gideon woke for the first time since the shooting.

It had been nearly eighteen hours of waiting, of hoping.

Of praying that by some miracle, he would come back to her.

She had tended him as best she could, fully recovered from the ordeal herself and having never felt stronger in her life.

Thanks to him.

She went to his bedside as his eyelids began to twitch. Leaning over him, she stroked his face, smoothed back the soft spikes of his blond hair. He leaned his face into her touch, moaning quietly. His eyes opened narrowly, squinting in the dim light of the shaded bedroom. "Where are we?"

"My sister's house," she answered gently.

He wheezed slightly, anxious now. "Are we alone? Does anyone know I'm here?"

"Just Amelie. It's okay, Gideon. She knows about you. I helped her understand what you are. She'll keep our secret."

"Where is she?"

"In the other room, watching television."

He turned his face toward the hallway wall, and Savannah guessed he was searching for Amelie through the extrasensory ability he possessed. "I can't see her. My talent...it's not working. It's gone."

Savannah could feel his agitation. His pulse spiked with it. He brought his hand up to shield his eyes. "So bright in here."

She glanced to the window blinds, which were drawn down and blotted out all but the most scant illumination from the afternoon sunlight outside. "I'm sorry. I thought it would be dim enough for you."

She walked over to the dresser and brought back a pair of bug-eye sunglasses. "Here," she said, carefully slipping them on his face. "Try these."

He opened his eyes and gave a mild nod of approval. "Better. Probably not my best look, though."

"You look pretty good to me." She smiled and sat down next to him on the mattress. "I wasn't sure you would wake up again. I wasn't sure it would work."

At his frown, she went on. "That night when you came back in such terrible shape from Keaton's place, your friend from the Order said you needed blood. And Amelie told me what you did for me last night, after I was shot. You saved me with your blood, Gideon. So, I had to try to save you with mine."

He blew out an oath. "The blood bond, Savannah...it's permanent. Unbreakable. It's a sacred thing." His frown deepened. "This isn't the way it's supposed to be."

She sat back, feeling hurt. Feeling she'd done something wrong and he was disappointed. "I'm sorry if it wasn't what you wanted."

Gideon pushed himself up off the bed, and groaned in pain.

"Be careful," she said, trying to ease him back down. "You shouldn't be moving around, and I shouldn't be saying things that upset you. You were shot last night too. The one that hit me passed cleanly through my lung and ribs, but the one inside you..."

"Still in my head," he guessed grimly. "In my brain."

Savannah gave him a sober nod. "Amelie wanted to take you to the hospital—"

"No." He said it firmly, the same way he'd insisted the other night in Boston when she wanted to get him medical help for his injuries then. "Human doctors can't help me, Savannah."

"I know," she said. "So, I did the only thing I could think of."

He reached out, took her hand in his. "You saved my life." He swore again, more roundly this time. "When I realized you'd left...when I knew Keaton's Master was still out there somewhere, I couldn't get to you fast enough, Savannah."

She heard the rage in his voice for the enemy he'd wanted so badly to root out and destroy, and she nodded sadly. "I'm glad he's dead. For what he did to Rachel and your brothers, even to Professor Keaton.

For what he did to you, Gideon, I'm glad Smithson is dead. I'm glad you got what you came here for."

He scowled. "I came for you, Savannah. I love you. I should've said it before. I should say it a thousand times now, so you'll know what you mean to me."

She felt a warmth blooming in her breast, seeping through her veins. Not her own emotion, but Gideon's. Flowing through their bond.

"I know you feel it," he said, his grasp warm on her hand. "I know you can feel my love inside you now, in your blood. Tell me you love me too, Savannah. Tell me you'll let me prove it to you. Be my mate. Come back with me to Boston. Let me try to be the hero you deserve."

She slipped her hand out of his and gave a small shake of her head. "I don't want a hero."

She thought about how he almost died last night—in combat, now with a bullet buried deep in his brain. A bullet that could dislodge anytime and wreak more damage, maybe something her blood wouldn't be able to fix.

Maybe the bullet already had taken things from him: His ESP talent. His eyes.

"I couldn't bear it," she murmured. "I can't stand by while you go out to war every night. I'm not strong enough to give you permission to fight and bleed and maybe never come back."

Gideon was silent for a very long while, his face downcast. "I've been killing Rogues nearly all my adult life, trying to even a score. Trying to atone. It was an empty quest. But the Order is my family, Savannah. The warriors are my brothers now, the only ones I'll ever have. I can't give them up, not even for you."

Her heart breaking, she nodded mutely. Struggled to find her voice. "I understand. It wouldn't be fair for me to ask that of you."

He lifted her chin on the edge of his hand. "You didn't. You asked me not to go out and fight. Maybe that I can do. Maybe there are other ways—non-combat ways—that I can serve the Order's missions, yet keep a pledge to you...my woman. My Breedmate. My forever love."

Savannah wanted to let her elation flood over her, but she was still stung by the way they'd left things back in Boston. "You hurt me, Gideon. You weren't honest with me. Without that, we'll have nothing."

"I know." He stroked her cheek. "I know, and I'm sorry. Let me make it up to you. Let me love you." He caught her nape in his big, strong hand and pulled her to him for a brief, tender kiss. "Say you love me, and let me start being the man you make me want to be."

She let out a sigh, unable to resist him or refuse him. "I do love you, Gideon."

"Then let me bond with you properly, the way I want it to be for you, for us. Be mine, Savannah."

"Yes," she whispered against his lips. "Yes, Gideon. I will be your mate."

He pulled her against him, letting her feel his arousal. "Let's make it right, now."

She reached out with her index finger to push the ridiculous sunglasses down on the bridge of his nose. Amber sparks shot through the pale blue of his eyes. "You're only a few hours out of death's doorway, and you want to make love?"

He grinned. "Oh, I want to do more than that."

"My sister is in the other room," she reminded him, whispering on a scandalized laugh.

Gideon was still for a moment, time during which the bedroom door quietly closed on its own volition, the lock softly clicking into place.

He kissed her, then trailed his lips along the side of her neck. Savannah's heartbeat throbbed in response to the subtle grazing of his fang tips at her pulse point. He dragged her farther up alongside him and rolled toward her, grinding his rigid length into her hip in invitation and demand.

"You're very bad," she said, as he opened his mouth over her carotid.

And then gently, sensually, she felt those razor-sharp points pierce her delicate skin. Her veins lit up, electric and hot with power, as Gideon drew the first deep swallow from her vein.

"Oh, God," she gasped, pleasure flooding her. "You are very, very bad."

And as her body melted into him, Savannah was thinking how a lifetime with Gideon was going to be very, very good.

~ * ~

ABOUT THE AUTHOR

LARA ADRIAN is the New York Times and #1 internationally best-selling author of the Midnight Breed vampire romance series, with nearly 4 million books in print worldwide and translations licensed to more than 20 countries. Her books regularly appear in the top spots of all the major bestseller lists including the New York Times, USA Today, Publishers Weekly, Indiebound, Amazon.com, Barnes & Noble, etc. Her debut title, Kiss of Midnight, was named Borders Books bestselling debut romance of 2007. Later that year, her third title, Midnight Awakening, was named one of Amazon.com's Top Ten Romances of the Year. Reviewers have called Lara's books "addictively readable" (Chicago Tribune), "extraordinary" (Fresh Fiction), and "one of the best vampire series on the market" (Romantic Times).

Writing as **TINA ST. JOHN**, her historical romances have won numerous awards including the National Readers Choice; Romantic Times Magazine Reviewer's Choice; Booksellers Best; and many others. She was twice named a Finalist in Romance Writers of America's RITA Awards, for Best Historical Romance (White Lion's Lady) and Best Paranormal Romance (Heart of the Hunter). More recently, the 2011 German translation of Heart of the Hunter debuted on Der Spiegel bestseller list.

With an ancestry stretching back to the Mayflower and the court of King Henry VIII, the author lives with her husband in New England, surrounded by centuries-old graveyards, hip urban comforts, and the endless inspiration of the broody Atlantic Ocean.

Visit the author's website and sign up for new release announcements at **www.LaraAdrian.com**.

Don't miss the ultimate insider's guide

The Midnight Breed Series Companion

Available now in paperback and ebook

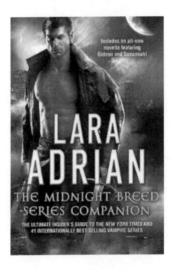

Never miss a new book from Lara Adrian!

Sign up for Lara's email newsletter at
www.LaraAdrian.com

Be the first to get notified of new releases and be eligible for special subscribers-only exclusive content and giveaways. Sign up today!

Complete list of titles by New York Times &
#1 internationally best-selling author
LARA ADRIAN

Midnight Breed Series
Kiss of Midnight
Kiss of Crimson
Midnight Awakening
Midnight Rising
Veil of Midnight
Ashes of Midnight
Shades of Midnight
Taken by Midnight
Deeper Than Midnight
A Taste of Midnight (ebook novella)
Darker After Midnight
Edge of Dawn
The Midnight Breed Series Companion
A Touch of Midnight (novella/series prequel)
Crave the Night (releasing early 2014)

NightDrake
A Glimpse of Darkness (ebook collaborative novella)

LARA ADRIAN writing as TINA ST. JOHN

Dragon Chalice Series
Heart of the Hunter
Heart of the Flame
Heart of the Dove

Warrior Trilogy
White Lion's Lady
Black Lion's Bride
Lady of Valor

Lord of Vengeance

Find Lara Adrian online at:

www.LaraAdrian.com

www.facebook.com/LaraAdrianBooks

www.twitter.com/lara_adrian

www.goodreads.com/lara_adrian

www.pinterest.com/LaraAdrian

www.wattpad.com/user/LaraAdrian

Made in the USA
San Bernardino, CA
05 June 2014